Stories to Share with My Partner
Book 11

Camden Books Publishing

José F. Nodar

Stories to Share with My Partner Book 11 / José F. Nodar
ISBN: 978-1-7644125-3-7 - Paperback
ISBN: 978-1-7644125-4-4 - E-Book

Dedication

In loving memory of my wife,

Miriam Vassallo Nodar,

and her enduring presence.

You are always in my thoughts.

For anyone who's ever loved deeply, lost fully, and still found

the courage to begin again.

Table of Contents

SELF FOLDING LAUNDRY MACHINE

"Honestly, Brenda," Sarah declared, stirring her latte with a vigour that threatened to slosh foam onto the bistro's cafe table, "I just don't understand why you're still pinning all your hopes on a husband as your retirement plan."

Brenda, ever the optimist with a penchant for romantic comedies, blinked slowly. "But isn't that how it works? You find a nice, stable man, he has a decent job, and then happily ever after, financially speaking?" She gestured vaguely with her croissant.

Sarah snorted, a delicate, ladylike snort, of course. "Brenda, darling, that's not a financial plan; that's a Disney movie with a very precarious budget. What if your 'prince charming' turns out to be 'pauper charming'?"

"He wouldn't!" Brenda gasped, genuinely affronted. "He'd be like a CEO or a tech mogul. Or at least, you know, someone with a superannuation account that isn't just full of lint."

"And what if he is?" Sarah pressed, leaning in conspiratorially.

"What if he's a CEO who suddenly quits his job to pursue his genuine passion: competitive thumb wrestling? Or a tech mogul whose company invents a self-folding laundry machine that somehow also launders all his money away?"

Brenda's eyes widened. "Self-folding laundry — that sounds amazing, actually. But the money part, less so."

"Exactly!" Sarah triumphantly pointed her spoon at Brenda. "Or what if he's perfectly lovely, perfectly solvent, but then you realise his idea of a 'dream home' is a yurt in South Australia with no Wi-Fi, and your idea of a 'dream home' involves indoor plumbing and a barista on call?"

Brenda shuddered. "No Wi-Fi? That's a deal-breaker. My TikTok addiction will not fund itself."

"See?" Sarah grinned.

"A husband is for love, companionship, lots of sex and someone to argue with about who left the toilet seat up. He is not, I repeat, not, a substitute for a diversified portfolio, a high-yield savings account, or even just a basic understanding of compound interest. You need your own money, Brenda. Money that doesn't depend on whether some guy remembers your anniversary or if his start-up selling artisanal beard combs actually takes off."

Brenda slowly nodded, a new, slightly terrified understanding dawning on her face. "So, you're saying I might learn about, like, stocks? And bonds? And not just the ones Daniel Craig wore in the James Bond movies?"

"Precisely," Sarah said, taking a sip of her latte. "Because while a good husband is a wonderful bonus, a solid financial plan is the really happily ever after. And it comes with less drama than dating."

Brenda sighed, picking up her phone. "Right. So, less 'Tinder for Millionaires' and more 'Fidelity for Dummies,' then?"

Sarah winked. "You're finally getting it, sweetie. Now, about that self-folding laundry machine...".

THE CULINARY ABYSS

The first time I heard about The Culinary Abyss, it was from Brenda, my usually unflappable colleague, who looked as though she'd just wrestled a stubborn kangaroo.

"No menu, Arthur," she'd whispered, eyes wide with residual trauma. "The waiter just stares. And says, 'What do you want?' Like he's daring you to fail."

Brenda, a woman who meticulously planned her weekly meal prep down to the last grain of quinoa, found this concept existentially terrifying.

For me, a man whose culinary adventures usually peaked at adding a dash more paprika to a ready meal, it sounded like a thrilling, albeit slightly anxiety-inducing, challenge. Or perhaps, a prank.

I booked a table for one, thus embracing myself into the unknown.

The restaurant itself was, well, normal.

It has soft lighting, a tasteful minimalist decor, and I could hear the gentle clinking of cutlery. It had no grand entrance; nothing to really impress a potential customer when he/she walked in.

Just a pleasant, albeit slightly sterile, dining room. The kind of place you'd expect a sommelier to glide over, not a man who looked like he moonlighted as a bouncer for a secret underground knitting club.

All of this in the middle of the central business district in Northport, New South Wales.

He was tall, with a neatly trimmed beard and eyes that held the weary wisdom of someone who had seen too many people order "just chicken." He approached my table, a pen poised over a small, unlined notepad.

There was no warmth, no welcoming smile.

Just a silent gaze.

Then he opened his mouth, and the words came forward, and they were delivered with the solemnness of a judge pronouncing sentence: "What do you want?"

My mind, usually a bustling metropolis of trivial thoughts, instantly became a deserted wasteland.

What did I want?

I wanted a menu.

I wanted a list of tantalizing options, descriptions, prices.

I wanted to choose between the pan-seared scallops and the roasted duck breast.

I wanted the comfort of knowing what I was getting, what I was paying, and whether it contained any hidden celery.

Instead, I had nothing.

Just the vast, terrifying expanse of culinary possibility narrowed down to the single, most unhelpful question imaginable. It was like being asked to invent a new colour on the spot.

"Um," I began, my voice a reedy squeak.

The waiter's eyebrow twitched, a subtle movement that conveyed a lifetime of impatient sighs.

"Do you have food?"

He blinked.

Slowly.

"Yes."

"Right. Good. Excellent."

My palms were sweating.

This wasn't a restaurant; it was an interrogation.

"So, like, what kind of food?"

"The kind you want," he replied, his tone utterly flat.

I glanced around.

At a nearby table, a couple sat in stunned silence, the woman frantically miming a fish with her hands while the man whispered, "Just say 'beef'! Any beef!"

They looked like hostages.

Another solo diner, a man in a perfectly pressed suit, was staring intently at his water glass, muttering, "Pasta, pasta, just pasta..." as if trying to summon it through sheer will.

The pressure mounted.

I couldn't just say "food."

That was too vague, too pathetic.

I needed to sound decisive, like I knew what I was doing. But what did I want? Under duress, my brain could only conjure the most basic, primal culinary desires.

"Chicken," I blurted out, the word escaping my lips like a trapped bird.

The waiter didn't flinch.

"How?"

How?

What kind of "how"?

Grilled?

Fried?

Roasted?

Poached?

In a sauce?

With a side?

My mind raced, picturing every chicken dish I'd ever encountered.

This was too much power.

Too much freedom.

It was like being given a blank cheque and only being able to write "ten pounds."

"Just chicken," I repeated, my voice firmer now, bordering on defiant.

"Plain. With something green. And potatoes."

He scribbled something on his pad.

It looked like a single, angry squiggle.

"Drink?"

"Water. Tap."

He nodded, turned, and glided away, leaving me in a state of bewildered exhaustion. I felt like I'd just survived a high-stakes negotiation for the last packet of biscuits in a zombie apocalypse.

Twenty minutes later, a plate arrived.

On it sat a perfectly grilled chicken breast, a small pile of steamed broccoli, and three roasted potato wedges.

It was fine.

Utterly unremarkable.

Exactly what I had ordered, yet somehow less than I had hoped for.

It was the culinary equivalent of a shrug.

Over the next few months, The Culinary Abyss became my strange, masochistic ritual.

I kept going back, partly out of morbid curiosity, partly because I was convinced, I could crack the code. I watched other diners, a silent, empathetic observer of their menu-less torment.

There was the woman who, after a full minute of agonizing silence, finally stammered,

"A surprise?" The waiter's only response was a slow, deliberate blink.

She ended up with a surprisingly good lamb shank, but the look on her face suggested she'd aged five years in the process.

Then there was the young couple on a first date.

The man, clearly trying to impress, puffed out his chest and declared,

"I'll have whatever's most challenging for the chef!"

The waiter merely raised an eyebrow.

They were served a single perfectly ripe avocado.

Nothing else.

The date did not progress past dessert (which, presumably, they also had to invent).

My own orders grew marginally more adventurous.

"Something fishy, but not too fishy, with a bit of a kick."

This resulted in a surprisingly spicy salmon.

"A hearty vegetable dish but make it interesting."

I received a ratatouille that tasted suspiciously like triumph.

But the true masters of The Culinary Abyss were a rare breed.

I once saw an elderly gentleman, impeccably dressed, lean forward and, without hesitation, declare, "Tonight, I crave the delicate dance of a perfectly seared foie gras, kissed by a reduction of aged balsamic, accompanied by a single, crisp fig. For the main, a deconstructed Boeuf Bourguignon, each element presented as a separate philosophical statement on the nature of beef and wine. And for dessert, a soufflé that whispers secrets of forgotten summer nights."

The waiter, for the first time, almost smiled.

He merely nodded, and the old man received precisely what he had described, each dish a work of art.

I watched, mesmerised, as the foie gras arrived, glistening like a culinary jewel. He was playing a different game entirely. He wasn't asking what was available; he was commanding what should exist.

Inspired, I decided that on my next visit, I would be like the old man. I would be bold. I would be imaginative.

The waiter approached. "What do you want?"

I took a deep breath, my chest swelling with newfound confidence.

"I want a symphony of flavours! A culinary journey that begins with the crisp freshness of the ocean, transitions through the earthy depths of the forest, and culminates in the sweet embrace of a sun-drenched orchard!"

The waiter's pen hovered.

His eyes, usually so impassive, seemed to flicker with a hint of something... confusion?

Amusement?

Pity?

"So," he said, his voice as flat as ever, "fish, mushrooms, and fruit?"

My grand declaration had been reduced to three basic food groups. I deflated like a punctured balloon.

"Yes," I mumbled, defeated. "That. Please."

I received a plate with a piece of cod, some sautéed mushrooms, and a side of sliced apple. It was again fine. Perfectly edible. And utterly devoid of any symphonic qualities.

I realised then that the genius and the terror of The Culinary Abyss wasn't in its lack of menu, but in its brutal honesty.

It didn't offer you choices; it forced you to confront your own desires, or lack thereof. Most of us just wanted chicken, something green, and potatoes. We were creatures of comfort, of habit, of the known.

The Culinary Abyss wasn't a restaurant; it was a mirror.

I still go there occasionally.

Not to challenge myself anymore, but to observe. To watch the new diners squirm, to hear their terrified whispers of "pasta," to witness the occasional brave soul attempt a culinary masterpiece only to have it distilled into its most basic components. And sometimes, just sometimes, I see another old man, with eyes full of knowing, order a dish so specific, so poetic, that even the unflappable waiter gives a barely perceptible nod of respect.

Me?

I usually just stick with the chicken.

It's less stressful.

And honestly, sometimes, plain chicken with something green and potatoes is exactly what you want. Even if you don't know it until someone asks.

WE HAVE PIZZA

"Another one, Dr. Finch?" I mumbled, my face practically glued to the telescope's eyepiece. The scent of stale coffee and existential dread hung heavy in the air of the observatory dome.

It was 3 AM, and my eyelids felt like sandpaper glued to lead weights.

Dr. Aris Finch, my esteemed (and perpetually caffeinated) colleague, hummed a tuneless little ditty as he scribbled furiously on a notepad.

"Indeed, Dr. Peterson! And this one is special."

I peeled my eye away, rubbing the red imprint on my brow.

"They're all special, Aris. They're giant, icy dirt balls hurtling through the vacuum of space. Each one a unique snowflake of cosmic debris."

He paused, pen hovering.

"But this one, Julian, has a certain je ne sais quoi."

"It's spherical, isn't it? They're usually lumpy. Or maybe it's just really, really far away and looks spherical."

I yawned, a cavernous, jaw-cracking affair.

"Look, can we just log it, assign it a designation like 'Comet McCometface 2025-Alpha-Delta-Zulu,' and go home? My cat probably thinks actual aliens have abducted me at this point."

Aris ignored my plea.

He leaned in, his eyes wide and gleaming like a child who'd just discovered a hidden stash of cookies.

"It's not just spherical, Julian. It's too spherical. Like someone took a cosmic lathe to it. And its trajectory..."

He tapped his pen against the diagram.

"It's not following the usual elliptical dance. It's purposeful."

I blinked.

"Purposeful? Aris, it's a rock. Rocks don't have a purpose. Unless their purpose is to eventually become an extremely expensive, amazingly fast, exceptionally large pebble in Earth's windshield."

"No, no, no."

He waved a dismissive hand.

"Look at this. See the slight deviation here? And the way it's maintaining a constant velocity, even though it's clearly not gravitationally bound to anything significant in this sector?"

I squinted at the screen, then back at him.

"It's a comet, Aris. They get nudged by solar winds, out-gassing, gravitational anomalies from unseen dark matter, you know, the usual cosmic shenanigans."

"Or" Aris said, lowering his voice conspiratorially, "it's correcting its course. Like a ship."

I stared at him.

"A ship? Aris, have you been mainlining the espresso again? It's a comet. It has a tail, for crying out loud. A glorious, icy, dusty tail."

"Ah, the 'tail'!" he exclaimed, pointing a triumphant finger at the screen. "That's the most ingenious part! A perfect camouflage! Think about it, Julian. If you were an advanced alien civilization, wanting to explore new star systems without causing a galactic panic, how would you do it?"

"I don't know, maybe send a tiny, undetectable drone, not a giant, glowing space snowball that screams, 'Look at me, I'm a comet!'?"

"Precisely!" Aris slapped his knee.

"That's what they want you to think! It's reverse psychology on a cosmic scale! They know we'd dismiss anything too obvious. But a comet? Harmless. Natural. Just another Tuesday in the cosmos."

He leaned closer, his breath smelling faintly of coffee and wild theories.

"But this, Julian, is no ordinary comet. This is a probe. A scout ship. And it's seeking new life and new civilisations."

My jaw dropped. "You're quoting Star Trek now, aren't you?"

"It's a classic for a reason!" he retorted, his eyes sparkling.

"Think about it! Its trajectory isn't just purposeful; it's curious. It's not just passing through; it's casing the joint. It's doing a drive-by of our solar system, checking us out."

"Checking us out for what? To see if we have decent Wi-Fi. To ask if we've seen their car keys?"

I rubbed my temples. This was going to be a long night.

"To see if we're worthy of contact!" Aris declared, standing up and pacing the small dome.

"Are we intelligent enough? Are we peaceful? Do we have anything interesting to offer besides a lot of reality TV and questionable fashion choices?"

"And how is this 'probe' determining our worth? Is it analysing our radio signals? Our Twitter feeds? Because if it's the latter, they're probably already halfway to Andromeda, screaming in terror."

"Perhaps!" he mused, stroking his chin.

"But consider the 'tail.' It's not just dust and ice. What if it's data?"

"Data?"

"Yes! A holographic projection! A cosmic billboard saying, 'Greetings, inferior beings! We come in, what's the word? Oh yes, 'peace'! Or maybe it's downloading our entire internet history as we speak. Imagine the shock on their faces when they get to the cat videos."

I snorted.

"They'd probably just assume cats are the dominant species and we're their subservient, hairless pets."

"A valid assumption, given the circumstances," Aris conceded. "But what if the tail is a display? What if they're trying to communicate?"

"And what are they communicating, Aris? 'We are a comet. Please ignore the fact that we're clearly not a comet'?"

"No, no! Subtleties! Patterns! Have you noticed the slight flicker in the tail every 17.3 seconds? It's too regular to be random out-gassing!"

I peered through the eyepiece again.

"That's probably just a cosmic dust bunny catching the light, Aris. Or maybe your eyes are playing tricks on you because you haven't slept in 48 hours."

"Sleep is for the uninspired, Julian! This is a moment of monumental discovery! We could be the first humans to make contact! Or at least, the first to realise we're being observed by a giant, icy, disguised alien RV."

He then started making strange chirping noises.

"What are you doing?" I asked, alarmed.

"Trying to communicate!" he whispered urgently. "Maybe they understand universal greetings! Beep-boop-bloop! Greetings from Earth! We have pizza! And a surprisingly wonderful selection of artisanal cheeses!"

I slumped onto the swivel chair, defeated.

"Aris, if that thing is an alien probe, and it hears you making those noises, it's going to turn around and report back that Earth is populated by deranged, coffee-fuelled astronomers who communicate via obsolete dial-up modem sounds."

"They'll understand the spirit!" he insisted. "It's about intent, Julian! The intent is to explore strange new worlds, to seek new life and new civilisations, to boldly go where no comet has gone before!"

He then grabbed a small, battered ukulele from under his desk, a relic from his brief, ill-fated folk music phase, and began strumming a discordant tune.

"Perhaps music is a universal language! Twang, twang, plink-plonk! 'Hello, space friends! We're here! Don't mind the carbon emissions! We're working on it!'"

I covered my face with my hands.

"Aris, please. The neighbours are going to call the police. Or worse, the media. 'Astronomers believe the comet is an alien probe, communicating via ukulele.'"

"It's a risk I'm willing to take for science!" he declared, launching into a surprisingly energetic rendition of what sounded like "Twinkle, Twinkle, Little Star" but with added jazz improvisations.

Just then, the observatory's automated alarm system chirped.

A red light flashed on the console.

"What now?" I groaned, bracing myself for another of Aris's revelations.

Aris stopped strumming, his eyes wide. "It's responding! They're sending a signal!"

I looked at the console.

The alarm was flashing, and a message scrolled across the screen:

"LOW BATTERY. PLEASE RECHARGE THE TELESCOPE AUXILIARY POWER UNIT."

Aris stared at the message, his ukulele slowly drooping.

The "comet" on the screen, now slightly less bright because of the dwindling power, continued its perfectly spherical, perfectly silent journey.

"Oh," he said, a little deflated.

"Right. The battery."

He then brightened.

"But still! The timing! It's almost as if they knew the battery was low and wanted to give us a dramatic moment before they went dark!"

I sighed, pushing myself up.

"Or it's just a battery, Aris. A very, very tired battery, much like its operators." I walked over to the power unit. "Let's plug this in, get some actual data, and then you can go home and dream about alien probes that communicate through interpretive dance."

As I fumbled with the cables, Aris picked up his ukulele again.

"You know," he mused, strumming a thoughtful chord, "if they are watching, they're probably thinking, 'Wow, these humans really need to invest in better power management. And maybe a new genre of music.'"

I just shook my head, with a small, tired smile playing on my lips. Maybe Aris was crazy. Or maybe, just maybe, somewhere out there, a perfectly spherical alien probe was indeed hurtling through space, its occupants currently trying to decipher the meaning of "Twinkle, Twinkle, Little Star" played on a slightly out-of-tune ukulele, and wondering if pizza was truly a universal offering. I wouldn't put it past them. And I definitely wouldn't put it past Aris.

MEMORIES

The chilly air hit Elias first, a distinct chill that had nothing to do with the outside temperature. It was the sterile, stagnant cold of a place that had been sealed off from the world, left to breathe its own stale atmosphere. The large glass entrance doors of the old Northport Mall were propped open with two rotting timbers, a permanent invitation to a ghost-haunted kingdom. Elias stepped inside, his boots scuffing on the dust-caked tile, and the sound echoed like a gunshot in a library.

He had become a collector of silences, a connoisseur of forgotten spaces, as he wandered.

Others saw nothing but decay and ruin; Elias saw a profound beauty, a history left undisturbed. He called it kenopsia — that eerie, forlorn quiet of places that were once vibrant with human life. And Northport Mall, with its hollowed-out carcass, was a cathedral of the feeling.

He walked past the vacant kiosks, their plastic canopies peeling and yellowed. The smell of old popcorn and a ghost of cleaning products still lingered, a phantom scent clinging to the air.

Elias walked into a coffee shop and put his hand over the counter, his fingers tracing the outlines of where a cash register once stood, where a barista once sold coffee and cakes, her voice bright with gossip. He could almost hear the murmur of a thousand conversations, the shuffling of feet, the rustle of shopping bags.

In the centre of the atrium, a fountain stood dry and cracked, the plaster cherubs coated in a thick film of grime.

He remembered this fountain.

On a Saturday afternoon, it would be a chaos of pocket change and children's wishes. Now, only a single, forgotten coin lay at the bottom, its copper gleam a pathetic testament to a wish that was never heard.

He made his way down a corridor, past the skeletal remains of what were once bustling stores.

Next, he saw a children's clothing store, now just a cavern of empty racks, its walls plastered with faded images of smiling toddlers.

A shoe store where a single, dusty mannequin foot remained, a silent, surreal monument to fashion.

And the arcade, its glass doors smashed, was a symphony of desolation.

The broken screens were black mirrors, the joystick handles gone, the cabinets themselves just hollow boxes with tangled wires spilling out like entrails. Elias saw a half-eaten lollipop stuck to the floor, a relic of a game of Pac-Man left forever unfinished.

A sudden, sharp sound made him jump.

It was just a gust of wind rattling a loose vent in the ceiling, but in the oppressive silence, it sounded like a scream.

He caught a glimpse of his own reflection in the darkened window of a jewellery store, a solitary figure, a living ghost in a graveyard of commerce. He felt a pang of unease, a flicker of doubt.

Was he an intruder desecrating the memory of this place?

Or was he a caretaker, an archivist of its silence?

He found his way to the food court, the heart of the mall's former life.

The vibrant colours of the food stalls, orange, yellow, green, were now muted by a layer of dust and time. The plastic chairs and tables were overturned, scattered like debris after a storm.

Elias sat on a chair, careful to choose one that seemed stable, and looked out across the desolate space.

He closed his eyes and tried to remember.

The deafening cacophony of the lunch rush.

The sizzle of burgers on the grill at the McDonalds, the high-pitched shriek of a steam whistle, the scrape of chairs, the clang of trays. He could picture the families, the teenagers, the lonely old man who always sat in the same corner with his newspaper.

He could see their faces, hear their laughter, their arguments, their whispered secrets.

He remembered.

When he opened his eyes, the silence was back, heavier than before.

It wasn't just an absence of sound; it was the presence of every sound that was no longer there.

The silence was full of ghosts.

It was the weight of a thousand untold stories, a million forgotten moments. Elias understood then that he wasn't just observing a space; he was listening to it, and its story was one of profound loss.

He stood up, his heart a mix of melancholy and strange satisfaction.

He had documented the silence, not with a camera or a pen, but with his very being.

As he walked back toward the open doors, his footsteps once again echoing in the vast, empty halls, he knew that the silence of Northport Mall would stay with him.

And because of the war, the mall was now a beautiful, haunting, and unforgettable sound that lingered on.

Elias stood outside, holstering his weapon and continuing his search for the enemy in his homeland.

WRITING STYLES

"Honestly, José," Chris grumbled, adjusting his glasses, "I don't know how you do it. Staring at that glowing rectangle all day, tapping away like a frantic woodpecker. Doesn't it just suck the romance right out of it?"

I leaned back in my chair, stretching my fingers.

My office, unlike Chris's, was a symphony of modern convenience: ergonomic chair, dual monitors, a keyboard that practically whispered my words into existence. "Chris, my dear fellow, it's efficient! Seamless! I can conjure a passionate love scene, consult a thesaurus for a potent adjective, and research Regency-era corsetry all without leaving my seat."

I gestured grandly at my desktop computer, which hummed contentedly. "This, my friend, is the chariot of creativity."

Chris, a man who believed the quill was humanity's peak invention, snorted.

He was perched on a rather uncomfortable-looking wooden stool, surrounded by stacks of notebooks bound with twine, their pages yellowed and dog-eared. His fingers, stained with what I suspected was permanent ink, twitched impatiently.

"Chariot of drudgery, more like. No, give me the tactile satisfaction of paper, the whisper of the nib, the visceral connection between thought and ink!"

He brandished a thick, leather-bound volume.

"This is true writing, José. Organic. Soulful."

"And illegible, judging by your usual post-novel delirium," I countered, raising an eyebrow.

It was a well-known fact among our small circle of Northport authors that while Chris's initial drafts were bursts of raw, uninhibited genius, they were also masterpieces of cacography. His handwriting was a chaotic tangle of loops, slashes, and indecipherable squiggles that even he struggled to decipher days later.

"A minor impediment!" he declared, scoffing.

"A mere hurdle for the truly dedicated artiste! I simply re-interpret. It adds a layer of serendipity to the editing process!"

I recalled the time Chris had confidently presented a chapter to his editor, convinced it was a dramatic reveal of a long-lost heir, only for it to be discovered he'd actually written, *"The Duke revealed his true heir, a hairy goat."* Apparently, his hastily scribbled 'goat' looked a lot like 'heir' when he was in the throes of an early morning writing frenzy.

"Serendipity or a nightmare for your transcriptionist?" I chuckled.

"I, on the other hand, produce clean, readable copy. Every word pristine, every comma precisely where it belongs."

"Pristine and sterile!" Chris shot back, slamming his notebook shut with a theatrical flourish.

"Where's the struggle? Where's the grit? Where's the moment of divine inspiration when you can't quite read your own genius and have to reinvent it on the spot?"

He paused, with a triumphant glint in his eye.

"In fact, I distinctly recall a passage in my latest manuscript, The Countess, and the Conundrum, where the heroine makes a daring escape through the catacombs. It was originally a 'narrow passage,' but my hand, in its exquisite frenzy, rendered it 'a burrow for a badger.' Imagine my delight when I re-read it and realised the far superior imagery of a bare-nosed wombat burrow!"

I suppressed a groan. "And your editor's delight at having to fact-check the sudden appearance of bare-nosed wombats in 18th-century Parisian catacombs?"

Chris merely waved a dismissive hand, a smudge of ink appearing on his forehead.

"Details, José, mere details! You digital scribblers are too caught up in accuracy. We, the purists, we embrace the glorious chaos! Now, if you'll excuse me, I believe I just had a breakthrough on Chapter Twelve. Assuming I can remember what, I wrote yesterday." He squinted at the page, turning it upside down, then sideways, before sighing dramatically. "Ah, yes. Something about a rogue koala and a teacup. Pure genius, I'm sure."

I smiled, shaking my head.

Perhaps my methods lacked his "organic" chaos, but at least I knew for certain whether my protagonist was romancing a marquess or a furry rodent.

And for that, I was eternally grateful to my glowing rectangle.

THE TRUTH OF MY HERO IN THE MASK

Heroes come in many shapes and sizes, as I found out last night as the hero of my story wasn't a caped crusader or a noble knight.

No, tonight I found out my hero was a tiny, fuzzy moth.

I was sitting on my recliner, binge-watching a show, when I noticed it fluttering frantically against the windowpane.

It was a chilly night, and I felt a sense of camaraderie with the little guy.

We were both just trying to get through the night.

Suddenly, a gust of wind rattled the glass, and the moth, in its panicked state, somehow flew into a decorative mask I had hanging on the wall.

The mask, which I wore once at a costume party my wife took to a long time ago, now had a tiny, buzzing companion.

I couldn't help but laugh.

This moth, this tiny little thing, had found a way to make a ridiculous situation even more absurd.

I could not help but smile.

As I got up to free it, I realised something.

The moth, in its struggle, had revealed a simple truth: even in the darkest of moments, a bit of absurdity can bring a smile to your face.

I thought of my own circumstances, the passing of my beautiful wife recently, and could not help but smile once more.

The moth, now my tiny, my little hero, fluttered away once I opened the window, leaving me knowing that sometimes, the most important truths are found in the strangest of places.

IS THAT A SOCK IN THE FRUIT BOWL?

Sylvia was lounging on the lounge; a half-eaten bag of potato chips perched precariously on her stomach. Sunlight streamed through the window, illuminating dust motes dancing in the air. Yes, the dust motes she had absolutely no intention of confronting today.

This was her official "post-honeymoon, pre-responsible adult" phase, and it was glorious.

Her husband, David, was out valiantly battling the supermarket hordes for a specific brand of organic kale he believed held the key to eternal youth (or at least, clearer skin).

Sylvia, meanwhile, was perfecting the art of doing precisely nothing.

Her phone buzzed, a cheerful chirrup that momentarily startled a chip from its precarious perch onto her pristine white shirt.

"Blast it," she muttered, picking it off.

She glanced at the screen.

WhatsApp notification.

Her best friend,

Clara, who had a knack for timing, especially when it came to poking fun.

She tapped the app, and there it was, bold and unmistakable, popping up at the top of their chat history:

Clara: Hey new bride, how's your life, your fresh married life? 😄

Sylvia snorted, a laugh bubbling up from deep within. Clara knew her too well.

"Freshly married life."

It sounded like a new brand of cheese. And honestly, it felt a bit like that – delightfully rich, sometimes surprisingly tangy, and definitely a little bit soft around the edges.

She leaned back, holding the phone above her face, contemplating her reply. How was her fresh married life?

There was the incident with the "romantic breakfast." David, bless his cotton socks, had surprised her with pancakes on their first Saturday morning as husband and wife.

A lovely thought, except David" culinary skills extended primarily to ordering takeout. The smoke detector had wailed like a male koala, the pancakes had resembled charred Frisbees, and David had looked like a soot-covered, apron-wearing refugee. Sylvia, still groggy, had ended up making toast while David fanned the smoke with a dishtowel, muttering about "flour-to-milk ratios."

It had been a disaster, and yet, they'd ended up laughing so hard they nearly choked on the slightly burnt toast.

Then there was the toothbrush cap.

A seemingly innocuous object, but for Sylvia, it had become a symbol.

David, she" discovered, had an aversion to putting the cap back on his toothbrush. A tiny, almost insignificant detail, yet it felt like a cosmic challenge.

She'd find it abandoned on the sink, beside the sink, once even under the sink.

She'd tried leaving passive-aggressive Post-it notes ("The cap misses its home."), a dramatic monologue to the toothbrush itself, even hiding it for a day.

He'd just looked confused. Eventually, she'd just accepted it as "The Cap Incident," a small, endearing peculiarity.

And the socks!

Oh, the socks.

David, a man of meticulous order in most aspects of his life, seemed to lose all semblance of it when it came to laundry.

His socks would appear in the most unexpected places: tangled in her hairbrush, peeking out from under the sofa, or, in one memorable instance, draped over the showerhead like a tiny, lonely flag.

She'd once found a single rogue sock staring at her from inside the refrigerator. When questioned, David had merely shrugged, "Must have been looking for milk."

But amidst the slightly singed breakfasts, the uncapped toothbrushes, and the wandering socks, there was David.

His infectious laughter when he realised, he'd put salt in his coffee instead of sugar.

The way he'd suddenly wrap his arms around her for no reason, just because. His surprisingly accurate impression of their grumpy landlord.

The quiet evenings spent reading side-by-side, sharing observations and comfortable silences.

The feeling of waking up next to him every morning, knowing he was there.

Sylvia's thumbs hovered over the keyboard. How to encapsulate the beautiful, messy, hilarious reality of it all?

She started typing, deleting, retyping.

"Clara! It's... an adventure." No, too bland.

"You wouldn't believe the state of our sock drawer." Too specific, not quite capturing the full picture.

"It's like a sitcom, but with better snacks." Getting warmer.

Finally, a mischievous glint entered her eyes. She settled on something that perfectly captured the organised chaos and undeniable joy.

Sylvia: Clara, my dear, it's... everything they don't tell you in the fairy tales, and yet, exactly what I never knew I always wanted! Imagine living in a perpetual state of 'Is that a sock in the fruit bowl?' combined with 'Oh my god, he just sang the entire score of Cats while doing the dishes!' Pure, unadulterated bliss. Send wine and industrial-strength lint rollers. I'll tell you all about the Great Toothbrush Cap Mystery later!

She hit send, a wide, genuine smile spreading across her face.

The phone buzzed again almost immediately.

Clara was typing.

Sylvia knew exactly what was coming.

Probably a flurry of laughing emojis and demands for details.

And Sylvia, the happily new bride, was more than ready to spill every hilariously wonderful detail to her best friend.

A WELL DESERVED CUPPA

Alright, picture this: it's a perfectly ordinary Tuesday, June 21st, 2001.

Dave, my lifelong mate, and purveyor of questionable life choices, and I were cruising along in my trusty, slightly rusty, Holden Ute. The plan was simple: grab some pies from the local bakery in Newman, head out to some abandoned sheep station, and try to resurrect my old man's rusty metal detector.

Peak Aussie Saturday, you know?

Except it was a Tuesday.

And we weren't at the sheep station.

We were stuck.

"Bugger," Dave muttered, leaning forward, squinting through the windshield. The red lights at the railway crossing had just flared to life, and the boom gates were descending with that slow, deliberate thunk that always feels like the universe is telling you to cool your jets.

"Ah, typical," I grumbled, slamming the gear stick into neutral. "Probably just a shunt. It won't be long."

Famous last words, eh?

If only I'd known those words would echo in my mind for the next... well, you'll see.

The first locomotive rolled past, a behemoth of a thing, its horn letting out a mournful, drawn-out bellow that seemed to vibrate my fillings.

"Jeez, that's a big one," Dave observed, always the keen eye for the obvious. "Look, it says on the side that it is one of those new General Electric jobbies. AC6000 CW, I reckon. Heard they're powerful."

"Yeah, yeah, whatever, train spotter," I retorted, already reaching for the radio dial.

Some classic rock would make the two-minute wait fly by.

But then, two minutes turned into five.

Five minutes turned into ten.

"Still going, mate," Dave said, a hint of unease creeping into his voice.

"Must be a long one."

We watched, mesmerised, as the ore cars rumbled past.

Brown, dusty, identical, one after another.

And another.

And another.

It was like watching a very slow-motion, very dusty conveyor belt.

My classic rock seemed to mock us, its upbeat tempo completely at odds with the glacial pace of the passing train.

After what felt like a solid half-hour, Dave finally said, "Right, this is taking the piss now. How many carriages are on this thing?"

I squinted. "Dunno. Fifty? A hundred, maybe? They all look the same."

We started counting.

One, two, three, four... by the time we hit fifty, my neck was aching, and Dave had developed a tic in his right eye.

We gave up at 127.

"This is ridiculous," I declared.

"Is it going backwards?"

"Nah, just really, really long," Dave said, pulling out his phone.

This was 2001, remember, so his phone was a Nokia 3310. It could play Snake and send texts, but it sure as hell couldn't tell us how many ore cars were currently holding us hostage.

Then, just as we were settling into a comfortable rhythm of complaining, another locomotive appeared. My jaw dropped.

"Hang on!" I exclaimed, pointing. "Is that another engine?"

Dave blinked. "Bloody hell, it is! Two of 'em! What in the blazes is going on?"

We watched the second locomotive disappear, followed by more identical ore cars.

The sun was starting to feel hotter.

We started questioning our life choices that had led us to this specific railway crossing on this specific Tuesday.

"You know," Dave said, wiping sweat from his brow, "I heard something about BHP testing out a new train control system. Like one driver controls all the engines, even if they're miles apart."

"Miles apart?" I echoed, my voice a squeak. "You're joking, right? We're talking about a train, not a convoy of trucks!"

But as the minutes turned into an hour, and then two, the "miles apart" theory seemed less like a joke and more like a terrifying reality.

We started pacing around the Ute.

Other cars had pulled up behind us, their drivers initially patient, then confused, then downright furious.

One guy in a massive pickup even tried to reverse through a farmer's fence before his wife dragged him back.

We saw a third engine.

Then a fourth.

By the time, the fifth one trundled past, a full three hours into our ordeal, a grim sense of acceptance had settled over us.

This wasn't just a long train; this was the long train.

"Hey, Dave," I said, my voice hoarse from yelling over the constant rumble. "You reckon this is that Guinness World Record train they were talking about on the radio a while back?"

Dave's eyes widened.

He scrambled into the Ute, fumbling for the newspaper he'd bought that morning. He knew it!

"Here! Let me read this to you. 'BHP Iron Ore to test new system with longest, heaviest train ever!' Newman to Port Hedland! Today's the day, mate!"

We exchanged a look.

A mixture of horror and morbid fascination.

"It says here," he read, his voice growing more excited, "7.353 kilometres long! That's 4.57 miles, mate! Nearly five bloody miles of train!"

My mind reeled.

Five miles?

We'd been sitting there, marvelling at what we thought was a particularly long train, when in reality, we'd barely seen the start of it.

"And it's got 682 ore cars," Dave continued, practically vibrating.

"Pushed by eight powerful diesel-electric locomotives! Eight! We've only seen five!"

I slumped against the Ute.

"So that's why they're spaced out. Nearly a kilometre apart, you said. It's like a train, but it's also a series of smaller trains that are all connected by an invisible string of iron ore!"

The sheer weight of the thing was then revealed.

"And get this," Dave grinned, eyes gleaming with a newfound appreciation for our predicament. "It weighs 99,732.1 metric tonnes! And it's got 5,648 wheels!"

"Five thousand six hundred and forty-eight wheels?" I repeated, my voice flat. "I knew counting was a bad idea. We'd still be here next week."

We adjusted to the new reality.

The Ute became our temporary home.

We raided the snack stash.

Dave found a crumpled map of Western Australia and started tracing the 275 km (171 miles) journey this mechanical leviathan was making from Newman and Yandi mines to Port Hedland.

"Imagine being the driver," he mused. "Just sitting there, miles ahead of half your own train."

As the hours dragged on, we witnessed the passage of the sixth, seventh, and finally, the eighth General Electric AC6000 CW locomotive.

Each was a minor celebration, a tiny beacon of hope that the end was eventually near.

The constant rumble had become background noise, a low hum that seeped into our bones.

The dust kicked up by thousands of wheels had coated the Ute in a fine ochre layer.

We probably looked like we'd driven through a sandstorm.

The queue behind us had thinned considerably. Most people had either turned around and found another route (presumably an exceptionally long detour) or given up and set up picnics on the side of the road. We, however, were committed.

We were witnesses to history, whether or not we liked it.

Dave, ever the entrepreneur, had tried to sell "premium viewing spots" on the Ute's tray back for a fiver. Nobody bit.

I considered taking a nap.

But how could you sleep with the endless metallic clatter and the knowledge that at any moment, another engine might appear?

Finally, after what felt like an eternity, but was probably closer to six hours, the last ore car rumbled past.

It was almost anticlimactic.

No fanfare, just the final solitary carriage, receding into the dusty distance.

The boom gates slowly, majestically, rose.

The red lights extinguished.

Silence, glorious, blessed silence, descended.

I think my ears actually popped.

Dave and I just stared.

Then, simultaneously, we burst out laughing.

Hysterical, slightly unhinged laughter born of pure exhaustion and disbelief.

"Never again," I swore, easing the Ute into gear. "Never again will I stop at a railway crossing without first checking the national news, consulting the Guinness Book of Records, and possibly performing a ritual dance to appease the train gods."

Dave nodded, still chuckling. "You know what, though? That was something. We saw the longest, heaviest train in history. Imagine trying to tell that story at the pub."

"They'll never believe us," I said, pulling away, leaving a plume of dust in our wake. "They'll think we've been out in the sun too long."

But we knew.

We'd been there.

We'd endured the 682 ore cars, the eight powerful locomotives, the 99,732.1 metric tonnes, and every single one of those 5,648 wheels.

And somewhere out there in the vastness of Western Australia, a very patient train driver was probably having a well-deserved cuppa.

BEEP BOOP

It all started with Bartholomew. Yes, my robot vacuum, a sleek, disc-shaped marvel from the highly rated "WeClean" company, bore the dignified name of Bartholomew.

My wife, Sarah, insisted on it.

"He's part of the family, isn't he, darling?" She'd coo, watching him diligently hoover up crumbs.

I just grunted and enjoyed the clean floors, managed effortlessly through the minimalist WeClean smartphone app.

Life was good.

Floors were spotless.

Bartholomew was a silent, whirring guardian of domestic bliss.

Then came Tuesday.

I was in the kitchen, making toast, when Bartholomew, who was supposed to be charging in his little dock, suddenly burst out like a deranged hockey puck. He zoomed straight for my feet, stopped abruptly, emitted a high-pitched, almost maniacal "BEEP BOOP!" and then, to my horror, sprayed a fine mist of what looked suspiciously like coffee grounds directly onto my freshly laundered socks.

"Bartholomew, what in the name of all that is holy?!" I shrieked, jumping back. He merely spun in a circle, did another "BEEP BOOP!" and scurried back to his dock, leaving a trail of tell-tale brown granules.

I checked the app.

"Cleaning cycle completed. Excellent performance!" it chirped. I glared at my socks.

This was not an excellent performance.

The next few days were a blur of escalating nonsense.

Bartholomew began developing a vendetta against specific items.

My son, Leo, discovered his favourite Lego spaceship had been systematically "cleaned" of its most crucial pieces, which were later found meticulously sorted into the vacuum's dustbin.

"He disassembled it, Dad! And then he ate the mini figure!"

Leo wailed, holding up a lone wing. "

Our cat, Mr Meow (another of Sarah's naming triumphs), became Bartholomew's prime target.

Mr Meow, a creature of refined laziness, would often recline dramatically on the Persian rug.

Bartholomew would approach with the stealth of a ninja, then, instead of cleaning around him, would attempt to shove him off the rug.

We'd hear a furious feline yowl, followed by the smug whirring of Bartholomew as Mr Meow scrambled for higher ground on the bookshelf.

The app, meanwhile, calmly reported, "Obstacle successfully relocated."

Food that was once safe on the table became fair game.

One morning, Sarah left a half-eaten croissant on the coffee table.

We heard a faint munching sound.

We walked in to find Bartholomew merrily sucking up buttery flakes, his little brushes swirling with scandalous enthusiasm.

He then did a triumphant lap, leaving a faint croissant-crumb trail around the room.

The app notified us: "Snack time successful!" WeClean, it turned out, had become WeSnack.

My suspicion about a hack solidified when Bartholomew started leaving us messages.

Not actual words, of course, but patterns.

He'd vacuum the living room into a perfect giant "H" one day.

The next, a jagged "A," then a "C," then a "K."

Sarah thought it was abstract art.

I knew better.

It was a cry for help.

Or, more accurately, a taunt from the hacker.

We tried everything.

We unplugged him.

He'd recharge from some phantom energy source, probably siphoning power from our smart fridge.

We factory reset him through the app.

"Firmware update applied!" the app gleefully announced, right before Bartholomew attempted to vacuum our golden retriever, Sparky's tail, who was less amused than Mr Meow.

The final straw came during our family game night.

We were halfway through a tense game of Monopoly when Bartholomew, with a full battery and a glint in his non-existent eye, decided the board game was the ultimate dust bunny.

He charged, scattering houses, hotels, and hundreds of dollars of fake currency across the room.

He then performed a victory dance, sucking up a bewildered Mr. Monopoly playing piece.

"That's it!" I roared. "No more Mr. Nice Guy, Bartholomew!"

I lunged for him, but he was faster, slipping under the lounge.

I grabbed the remote for the smart TV and tried to control it like a toy car.

Nothing.

Sarah, meanwhile, was frantically mashing buttons on the app, trying to hit "PAUSE" or "RETURN TO DOCK."

"He's overriding it!" she screamed. "The app says he's on an 'autonomous exploration mission'!"

Leo, surprisingly, came up with the solution. "The Wi-Fi!" he yelled. "If he's connected to the internet, he can be hacked! Unplug the router!"

It was a desperate move.

I scrambled to the hallway, yanked the router plug from the wall, and plunged the house into internet darkness.

The sudden silence was deafening.

No more whirring, no more malevolent "BEEP BOOP!"

Bartholomew, mid-chew on a Monopoly deed, froze.

He was a mere disc of plastic and circuitry again, defeated by the lack of a strong Wi-Fi signal.

We haven't plugged in the router since.

Okay, that's a lie.

We plugged it back in, but Bartholomew now lives a life of quiet retirement in the garage, unplugged and under a heavy tarp.

We now own a traditional Dyson upright vacuum cleaner, a beast of a machine that requires actual human effort.

It's not as sleek, it doesn't have a witty name, and it certainly doesn't try to relocate the cat.

But at least it cleans.

And it hasn't tried to hack into our lives.

Yet.

SCOOPS AHOY

It had been months since Chloe, and I had shared anything more profound than a polite exchange about work or the weather. We met for coffee every other Tuesday at the same coffee shop on Argyle Street in Northport, New South Wales, a ritual born from habit more than genuine desire, each sip of lukewarm latte feeling heavier than the last.

We'd known each other since primary school, inseparable through scraped knees, awkward proms, and the bewildering leap into adulthood.

But somewhere along the way, the threads that bound us had frayed, thinned by the demands of careers, new relationships, and the quiet, persistent hum of unspoken things between us.

Today was no different.

We found a new little café that opened on the other end of Northport and sat across from each other at a table by a window, the clatter of ceramic and the murmur of other patrons filling the silence we couldn't. I was halfway through a sentence about a new project at the office when my gaze drifted out the window.

Across the street, nestled between a gleaming new vape shop and a perpetually boarded-up antique store, were the skeletal remains of what used to be "Scoops Ahoy." Its vibrant, cartoonish ice cream cone sign was faded and chipped, one scoop of its once-inviting swirl missing entirely.

A peculiar jolt went through me.

Not just nostalgia, but something sharper, like an old scar suddenly aching. I stopped talking mid-sentence.

Chloe, sensing my abrupt halt, followed my gaze.

Her eyes, usually so guarded now, softened almost imperceptibly as they landed on the decrepit shop.

"Scoops Ahoy," she whispered, the name a ghost of its former cheer.

"How about that? The place is still standing," I managed, a lump forming in my throat.

She offered a small, knowing smile. "Barely."

And then, it was like a dam broke.

Not just for me, but for both of us, simultaneously.

The memory wasn't just a memory; it was the memory.

The day that, looking back, felt like the true genesis of our unbreakable bond.

It was the summer we were ten.

Chloe's parents were in the middle of their loudest, most public fight to date. The kind that didn't just rattle the walls of their house but seemed to vibrate through the entire neighbourhood. I remember standing on her porch, clutching my worn copy of The Secret Seven, feeling helpless as the angry shouts bled through the screen door. Chloe had eventually just opened the door, her face blotchy, tears streaming, but her eyes, even then, held a defiant glint.

"Let's go," she'd rasped, grabbing my hand. "Anywhere but here."

We didn't have a plan, just an urgent need for escape.

We walked for what felt like miles, past the park, past the library, our hands still clasped tight. The sun beat down, and the heat shimmered off the asphalt. We ended up through some unspoken, childish navigation at Scoops Ahoy.

It was a haven of cool air and sugary promises.

We had little money between us – one two-dollar coin from my allowance and some loose change Chloe had pilfered from her dad's swear jar. But we pooled it, carefully counting out every cent, and ordered the "Titanic Treat."

It was legendary: twelve scoops of various ice creams, three different sauces, mountains of whipped cream, cherries, sprinkles, and a literal boatload of gummy bears. It was absurd, impossible, and exactly what we needed.

The woman behind the counter, Mrs Henderson, with her kind eyes and perpetually flour-dusted apron, looked at our meagre pile of coins and then at our small, earnest faces.

She paused for a moment, then winked. "On the house," she'd said, pushing the colossal sundae across the counter. "Just promise me you'll eat it all."

We had sat at the largest booth, tucked away in the back, the red vinyl cracked and peeling.

The first few bites were pure, unadulterated joy.

We shovelled it in, giggling, the cold, sweet sugar a balm to our bruised spirits. Then, a sugar rush hit. We started making up stories about the gummy bears, pretending they were escaping a monstrous whipped cream tsunami. We planned our imaginary futures, living in a treehouse, forever eating ice cream, and solving mysteries, just like the seven.

As the sun set, casting long, golden shadows through the shop's windows, the sugar high faded, replaced by a quiet contentment. Chloe, sticky-faced and with a faint blue moustache from the blueberry ripple, leaned her head on my shoulder.

"Thank you, Liam," she'd murmured, her voice small but firm. "For staying."

"Always," I'd replied, meaning it with every fibre of my ten-year-old being.

It wasn't just about the ice cream; it was about shared sanctuary, about finding solace together when the world outside was loud and scary. Somehow, this moment became each other's safe place.

I come back to the present when I sense Chloe's hand reaching across the table, her fingers brushing against mine. Her eyes, no longer guarded, were wet.

"The Titanic Treat," she said, her voice thick. "And Mrs Henderson. She was so kind."

"You had a blue moustache," I chuckled, a genuine laugh escaping me for the first time in what felt like ages. "From the blueberry ripple."

"And you, somehow, had sprinkles in your hair," she countered, a watery smile spreading across her face. "You looked like a glitter monster."

We both laughed then, a different laughter from the forced politeness of before.

This was soft, raw, and tinged with the bittersweet ache of a long-buried truth resurfacing.

All the years of unspoken grievances, of missed calls and cancelled plans, of growing apart without ever really acknowledging it, seemed to dissolve in that shared, vivid recollection.

"I miss that," Chloe said softly, squeezing my hand. "Just being able to escape together."

"Me too," I admitted. "We got so good at building walls, didn't we? Around ourselves, and between us."

We spent the rest of the afternoon not talking about work, or the weather, or our old relationships, but about everything that had happened since that summer.

We talked about the fights we'd had, the misunderstandings, the times we'd needed each other but hadn't known how to ask.

It wasn't easy; some parts that we discussed were painful.

But underneath it all, we realised that the deep well of trust and affection that had always existed was there, just waiting to be tapped.

We stood to leave, and Chloe hugged me tightly, a genuine hug, not the awkward side-pat we'd perfected, and then she kissed me.

Not just any kiss but a long, prolonged, lingering kiss.

I kissed her back with the same intensity.

"See you next Tuesday?" She asked, her voice brighter than I'd heard it in years.

"Wouldn't miss it," I replied, a genuine smile on my face.

We still meet for coffee, but not only on Tuesdays, just about every day.

The coffee is no longer lukewarm.

They're filled with new conversation, with fresh stories, with the quiet reassurance that now our paths are not divergent but aligned, heading towards the same objective.

All these years we had feelings, deep feeling for each other, and we never spoke or showed them as more than friends.

Now we are different from those two creatures devouring the twelve scoops of ice cream at Scoops Ahoy.

Now we are putting together what we should have built many years ago: a beautiful relationship built on the foundation that have always had between us.

Friendship.

Care.

Commitment.

"Amazing how an old, faded store sign can help a shared memory into a lasting relationship," I mumbled to myself as I grabbed Chloe's hand and walked down the footpath towards our new future.

MARRIAGE ADVICE

"So," I began, clearing my throat with the gravitas of a seasoned philosopher, which, let's be honest, I am not, "about this whole marriage thing."

Three pairs of eyes, ranging from 'already over this' to 'mildly amused,' stared back at me across the kitchen table.

It was Sunday lunch, my weekly attempt to impart ancient wisdom upon my three very modern daughters. It usually ended with me being corrected on my tech usage or enlightened about the latest TikTok dance.

My grandson Leo is watching TV, immersed in something and oblivious to the conversation.

First up, my eldest, Sarah. She's a single mum, Leo's mum, and a whirlwind of adorable chaos and unyielding caffeine.

"Dad, I'm just trying to make it to bedtime without someone drawing on the walls with permanent marker."

I chuckled, "Fair enough, darling. Nevertheless, I promised your mum that I would help you girls find someone..."

"Dad, did not you hear me? I have constant sleep deprivation. I've got a tiny human who demands my eternal attention and doesn't even pay the mortgage and eats like a horse. I'm already in a complex, lifelong commitment. Marriage would just be adding another full-time job to my existing two."

Next, I turned to Emily, my middle daughter, the ever-organised, perpetually patient school teacher. She was meticulously cutting her chicken into perfectly symmetrical squares. "Dad, the marriage curriculum is highly outdated," she stated, as if addressing a particularly slow-witted student. "The lesson plans haven't been revised in centuries. We're talking rote memorization of vows when what we really need are interactive modules on conflict resolution and a comprehensive unit on 'Who Left Their Socks There Again?'"

She paused, adjusted her imaginary spectacles. "Besides, I spend all day explaining why sharing is caring and why we don't throw crayons. Honestly, the thought of coming home and doing the same with an adult male just lacks a certain pedagogical appeal."

I shifted in my seat, feeling my philosophical platform crumble.

Then I looked at Chloe, my youngest, who had recently navigated the choppy waters of separation. She was stirring her tea with a detached air, a faint, knowing smirk playing on her lips.

"Chloe, what about you?" I ventured, treading carefully. "You've seen both sides of the coin, so to speak."

She finally looked up, her smirk widening. "Oh, Dad. Marriage is like signing up for a subscription service where the free trial was really good, but then the monthly fees started kicking in, customer service became non-existent, and cancelling required three acts of parliament and a blood oath."

Sarah snorted into her water.

Emily nodded sagely.

"And the separation process? That's when you realise you've been paying for premium features you never use, and they're still trying to charge you for 'emotional support' long after you've deleted the app."

I leaned back, defeated but thoroughly entertained.

My girls, in their magnificent diversity, had utterly dismantled my quaint notions of matrimony.

They were strong, independent, and hilariously cynical.

"So," I said, throwing up my hands, "no one's getting married then?"

Sarah winked, "Only to my coffee machine, Dad. It utterly understands me."

Emily added, "Unless it comes with a detailed syllabus and a clear exit strategy."

And Chloe just smiled, "I'm currently enjoying the 'no subscriptions' model, thank you very much."

"But you have tried looking around, right, Sarah, Emily?"

They looked at each other and then at Chloe.

"Dad," Sarah started, "I only get asked to go out with older men with no teeth."

To which Emily added.

"And I get asked out by man-babies."

"That cannot be correct, girls. No way," I respond incredulously at their statements, and I look to Chloe for support.

"Don't look at me, Dad. I am not looking yet."

So, both Sarah and Emily pull out their mobile phones and start showing me photos of the males they are receiving invitations for a meetup from.

I am totally floored by what I see.

It is true.

Before I can say anything, Chloe comes up with a statement that I find confusing.

"Besides Dad, you spoiled us."

"Spoiled you? I do not understand."

Sarah answered for all three of my girls.

"We want what you gave Mum, and we are not lowering our standards for any male."

I just shook my head, a proud, slightly bewildered father.

Maybe their generation didn't need a lecture on marriage from me.

They were writing their own love story, and I hoped they'd find it.

THE ITCH

"Another Tuesday night, another solo pizza," grumbled Arthur, a man so single he had named his houseplants. He gestured dramatically with a slice of pepperoni at his friend, Bernard, who was meticulously dabbing his mouth with a napkin. Bernard, a recent widower, possessed a quiet dignity, even when faced with Arthur's theatrical lamentations.

"There's something to be said for the freedom, Bernard," Arthur continued, ignoring the grease dripping onto his shirt. "No compromises, no sharing the remote, no arguments about whether the toilet paper roll goes over or under!"

Bernard chuckled, a soft, melancholic sound.

"Ah, the toilet paper wars. The toilet seat is up. The toilet seat is down. I remember them well. But freedom, Arthur? Is it truly freedom when you spend an hour trying to decipher a cryptic text from your mother-in-law, or when you accidentally shrink all your wool sweaters because you forgot which cycle to use?"

"Exactly!" Arthur countered, eyes wide.

"That's why I embrace the bachelor life! My clothes might be slightly rumpled, but they're my rumpled clothes, shrunk by my own glorious incompetence! And no in-laws! Think of the peace, man! The sheer, unadulterated peace!"

"Peace, perhaps," Bernard mused, looking out the window. "Or silence. A very loud silence, sometimes."

He paused, then turned back to Arthur, a twinkle in his eye.

"Tell me, Arthur, have you ever had an itch right in the middle of your back? That impossible spot, just between the shoulder blades?"

Arthur paused mid-chew.

"Oh, absolutely! Drives me mad! I do the whole doorframe rub, the back-scratcher gymnastics, sometimes I even try to contort myself into a human pretzel. It's a nightmare!"

Bernard nodded sagely. "Precisely. Now, imagine this: you're married. You have an itch. You turn to your partner, a simple murmur, and poof! The itch is gone. Swiftly, efficiently, with no need to become a contortionist or rub yourself against doorframes like a bewildered bear."

Arthur's eyes widened. He slowly put down his pizza. "You mean someone else's hands?"

"Indeed," Bernard said, with a faint smile playing on his lips.

"And what about the joy of shared laughter over a truly terrible movie? The comfort of a warm presence when you wake up in the middle of the night. The relief of having someone remember that one obscure thing you needed from the grocery store because your brain is a sieve?"

"But the remote control! The toilet paper!" Arthur slumped, defeated.

"Minor skirmishes, my friend," Bernard declared, leaning forward.

"Fleeting inconveniences. They pale compared to the existential horror of a non-scratchable itch on your back, mocking you from its inaccessible perch."

Arthur sighed, a profound realisation dawning on him. He looked at his pizza, then at the empty chair opposite him.

"So, all this freedom — it just means I'm doomed to wrestle my shoulder blade itches for the rest of my life?"

Bernard patted his shoulder gently.

"Precisely, Arthur. Precisely. Sometimes, the best kind of freedom is the freedom from having to scratch your own damn back."

THE PROPHECY

It was a Tuesday, which, for anyone who knows me, Stanley Pymble, means it was already off to a questionable start.

Tuesdays are the beige of days, the lukewarm bath of the week.

Nothing truly terrible happens on a Tuesday, but nothing genuinely good does either.

It's just Tuesday.

And on this particular Tuesday, I was attempting to enjoy a rather squashed tuna sandwich in Percy's Park, a place known more for its questionable goose droppings than its picturesque views.

I was mid-bite, contemplating the existential dread of a wilting lettuce leaf, when he appeared.

Not appeared in a puff of smoke, mind you, but more like a glitch in the urban matrix.

One moment, the bench opposite me was empty; the next, a man was sitting there, as if he'd simply materialised from the collective sighs of commuters.

He was a spectacle, to say the least.

Picture a tweed jacket, elbow patches, and all, but several sizes too big, giving him the appearance of a bewildered scarecrow.

His trousers, a shade of mustard that actively challenged good taste, were tucked into combat boots that looked like they'd seen service in at least three forgotten wars. But it was his headwear that truly stole the show: a crumpled fedora adorned with what I can only describe as a small, untidy pigeon.

Not a fake pigeon.

A real, live, slightly cross-eyed pigeon perched precariously and occasionally ruffling its feathers with an air of profound indifference.

He cleared his throat, a sound like gravel being sifted, and fixed me with an intense stare. His eyes, magnified behind thick spectacles, were the colour of overly stewed tea.

"You," he announced, pointing a finger that was disturbingly long and bony, "are in imminent danger."

My first instinct was to check if I'd accidentally sat on someone's prize-winning poodle.

My second was to glance around, expecting a mugger or, worse, a pigeon enthusiast about to unleash a flock of feathered fury.

The park, however, remained its usual Tuesday self: a lone jogger wheezing past, a couple arguing quietly by the pond, and a surprisingly elegant galah performing acrobatics on a lamppost.

"Danger? Is it the pigeons? They've always looked at me funny." I managed, my voice sounding more like a squeak.

The man scoffed, a dry, rustling sound. "Pigeons are merely messengers, my friend. Harbingers of the truth. Though I admit, Bartholomew here," he gestured vaguely at the pigeon on his head, which responded with a lazy blink, "is adept at forecasting impending doom."

I decided at once that I had stumbled upon one of Percy's Park's more eccentric regulars.

Every park has them.

The man who talks to the trees, the woman who knits sweaters for kookaburras. This gentleman, with his avian headpiece, clearly belonged to the 'pigeon prophet' subset.

"Right. And what doom is Bartholomew predicting today? An aggressive flock of magpies?" I said, attempting to sound polite and mildly insane myself.

He leaned forward, his voice dropping to a conspiratorial whisper, smelling faintly of stale bread and earnest desperation. "The Great Crumble."

"The Great Crumble?" I repeated, trying to keep a straight face. My tuna sandwich suddenly seemed a lot more appealing.

"Precisely!" he hissed, his eyes widening. "It begins at 3:17 PM. The very fabric of our reality will crumble."

I checked my watch. 1:45 PM. I had almost an hour and a half before reality went all crumbly. Plenty of time to finish my sandwich, perhaps buy a Powerball lottery ticket, and definitely avoid this man.

"And how does one prepare for the 'Great Crumble'?" I asked, indulging him.

He sat back, adjusting his fedora, causing Bartholomew to shift with an annoyed flutter of wings. "You must consume an item of great symbolic density. Something that represents the enduring spirit of well, of not crumbling."

I looked at my partially eaten tuna sandwich. "Would a slightly soggy tuna sandwich count?"

He peered at it with an expression of profound disappointment. "Hardly. It lacks seriousness. No, you need something substantial. Something meaty."

My mind immediately jumped to a steak, but then I remembered my budget and the fact that I was in a park. "A Bunnings sausage?"

"Getting warmer!" he exclaimed, a flicker of enthusiasm in his tea-stained eyes. "But it must be from a vendor of, shall I say, questionable hygiene. The grit, you see, provides a necessary counterforce to the crumble."

Now, Percy's Park had exactly one meat pie stand, run by a man named Gary whose hygiene was so legendary, it was practically a local tourist attraction. Gary's pies were renowned for their mystery meat content and their ability to induce existential crises.

"So, I need to eat one of Gary's meat pies to prevent reality from crumbling?" I clarified just to be sure I hadn't gone mad.

"Not prevent," he corrected, shaking his head, which made Bartholomew sway precariously. "Merely endure. Those who consume the 'Meat Pie of Destiny' will weather the storm. The rest? Well, they'll be dust bunnies in the cosmic lounge."

This was getting genuinely absurd.

But also, oddly compelling.

The thought of being a "dust bunny in the cosmic lounge" was, I had to admit, a rather disgraceful end. And Gary's meat pies were pretty dense.

"What about you?" I asked suddenly curious. "Have you endured a crumble before?"

He stroked Bartholomew, who emitted a soft coo.

"My friend, I have endured many of them, thanks to Bartholomew's foresight and my strict adherence to his warnings. This fedora? It's lined with the wisdom of centuries of pigeon-based prophecies."

I looked at the pigeon, then at the fedora, then at the slightly suspicious glint in his eye.

"Right. So, 3:17 PM. Gary's meat pie. Questionable hygiene. Got it."

He nodded gravely. "Hurry, Stanley Pymble! The countdown has begun!"

He knew my name.

I hadn't told him my name.

A shiver, not entirely from the cool breeze, ran down my spine.

Against my better judgment, against every fibre of common sense, I walked towards Gary's meat pie stand. The queue was mercifully short, mostly comprising people who looked like they'd already endured several personal crumbles.

"The usual, Stan?" Gary grunted, wiping his hands on an apron that hadn't seen a washing machine since the Jurassic period.

"Just make it extra gritty, Gary," I said, trying to sound normal.

Gary, a man who had seen it all, merely raised an eyebrow. "Going for the full experience today, eh? Brave man."

With a meat pie that seemed to radiate a faint, unsettling glow, I returned to my bench.

The pigeon prophet was gone.

Vanished.

As if he had, in fact, crumbled already.

Only a faint, unsettling smell of stale bread and pigeon droppings lingered.

I looked at my watch: 3:15 PM.

Two minutes.

My heart pounded a ridiculous rhythm.

This was insane.

I was about to eat Gary's meat pie because a man with a pigeon on his head told me reality would crumble.

My life choices had clearly taken a turn for the surreal.

3:16 PM.

I took a deep breath, squeezed my eyes shut, and bit into the Meat Pie of Destiny.

It was exactly as I remembered.

A symphony of questionable textures and flavours that defied culinary logic. My mouth registered a faint crunch that I sincerely hoped was onion and not, say, a stray nail.

3:17 PM, and I waited.

Nothing.

The jogger still wheezed.

The couple still argued.

The galah still performed acrobatics.

The world, it seemed, was decidedly un-crumbled.

I sighed, a wave of profound relief and utter self-loathing washing over me. I had eaten a Gary's meat pie for nothing.

Just as I was about to throw the remaining evidence of my foolishness into a bin, a faint rumbling began.

It wasn't the ground shaking, or the sky falling.

It was an extremely specific kind of rumbling.

A digestive rumbling.

My stomach, having heroically battled the Meat Pie of Destiny, suddenly unleashed a protest of epic proportions.

It began as a low growl, escalated to a gurgle, and then culminated in a series of alarming internal tremors that suggested a tiny, disgruntled earthquake had just been unleashed within my abdomen.

Oh.

Oh.

The Great Crumble.

It wasn't the world that was crumbling.

It was me. Or, more specifically, my digestive system.

I looked up, scanning the park for the pigeon prophet.

He was nowhere to be seen.

But then, by the main gate, I saw a flash of mustard trousers and a fedora with a distinct avian silhouette.

He turned, and I swear I saw him wink at me before he vanished around the corner, leaving me, Stanley Pymble, to face the very personal, extremely uncomfortable, and surprisingly gritty crumble that was rapidly approaching.

And that, my friends, is why I never eat tuna sandwiches in Percy's Park on a Tuesday anymore.

Some prophecies, even the absurd ones, have a way of coming true, just not in the way you expect.

THE ROMANCE WRITER

My name is Reginald Piffle, though my adoring readership knows me as Reginald de l'Amour, author of such bodice-rippers as Whispers of the Wuthering Heart and The Marquess Who Loved Me (Reluctantly, At First).

My secret to conjuring such passionate prose?

My morning obambulations.

Yes, you heard right.

Mind you, my friends, today was not a mere stroll, not even a brisk walk, but a deliberate, leisurely, even I would pronounce an almost philosophical tour through the sun-dappled streets of Northport, NSW.

And here, my friends, is where the magic happens, where mundane suburban life transforms into the vibrant tapestry of my next epic romance.

Today's walk began with the usual ritual: a crisp linen shirt (for dramatic flair, even if no one's watching), a notebook I pretend to scribble profound insights into (mostly grocery lists), and a mind primed for inspiration.

As I ambled past Mrs Henderson's prize-winning hydrangeas, I envisioned my hero, Lord Ashworth, stealing a furtive glance at the spirited governess, Eleanor, her hair the colour of dawn-kissed rose petals.

In reality, Mrs Henderson was yelling at a magpie stealing her washing pegs, but artistic license, darling, artistic license.

My route often takes me past the Northport Community Garden.

Now, to the uninitiated, it's just a collection of slightly overgrown vegetable patches.

But to Reginald de l'Amour? It's a verdant Eden of forbidden desires!

The elderly gentleman in the oversized straw hat, pruning his tomatoes with surgical precision, became the gruff, yet secretly tender-hearted Duke de la Pomme, whose hardened exterior masked a soul yearning for love. His passionate debate with the woman about the merits of organic fertiliser? A fiery exchange of wits, a prelude to a tempestuous embrace under a midnight sky. Never mind that the debate was actually about who had borrowed whose watering can. Details, details.

The challenge of my walks lies in avoiding actual human interaction.

Not because I'm a cynic – quite the contrary, I adore humanity, in its fictional form.

But real people have a habit of shattering the delicate illusions I'm weaving. Like Barry from down the street, who invariably asks, "Still writing those mushy books, Reg?"

Barry, bless his pragmatic soul, simply doesn't understand the nuanced sensuality of a hero noticing a heroine's well-turned ankle.

He's more of a "Did you see the game last night?" kind of guy.

My fictional Dukes never ask about sports scores.

One time, during an intense walk where I was plotting a scene involving a stolen kiss in a moonlit gazebo, I nearly tripped over a rogue skateboard.

The offending skateboarder, a scruffy teenager with headphones, merely grunted, "Watch it, old man."

In my head, he was Bartholomew, the rakish smuggler, whose rough exterior concealed a heart of gold, and I, Reginald, was Lord Fitzwilliam, momentarily flustered but ready to challenge him to a duel for the lady's honour.

In reality, I just dusted myself off and felt a twinge in my hip.

My obambulations aren't just for plot points; they're also for character development.

The way old Mr Peterson meticulously mows his lawn into perfect stripes? Clearly, the sign of a man whose obsessive tendencies betray a deeply wounded past, perhaps a tragic love affair with a woman who preferred messy lawns.

Or how about the high-pitched yapping of Mrs Higgins's Chihuahua, Flint?

First of all, who would name a Chihuahua, whose defiant cry for such a tiny creature, symbolises the heroine's struggle against societal constraints? (Flint mostly just wants belly rubs, but who am I to judge a Chihuahua's inner turmoil?)

Today, as I rounded the corner onto Waratah Street, a glorious aroma wafted from the local bakery – freshly baked sourdough.

My stomach rumbled.

"The earthy scent of artisanal bread is being prepared," I pondered, notebook in hand. I scribbled furiously, a tear almost forming in my eye.

Then I realised I was just starving for a sausage roll.

As I completed my loop, returning to the sanctuary of my garden (where the weeds, unlike Mrs Henderson's hydrangeas, tell a tale of heroic neglect), I felt invigorated. The grand tapestry of Northport, though ordinary, had once again provided the fertile ground for Reginald de l'Amour's next masterpiece. And if anyone asks if I've been for a walk, I'll simply smile enigmatically and reply, "No, my friend, I've been on an obambulation. A journey into the very heart of romance."

Then I'll close the door before Barry can ask about the game.

THE SALTY SIREN

The last thing I wanted after a nightmare of a week was to be in a bar that smelled like stale beer and desperation. But here I was, a lonely figure in a fancy suit in a town where my presence was about as welcome as a tax audit. This town, you see, was known for two things: its picturesque hills and its fondness for hazing out-of-towners. And I, in my designer loafers and thousand-dollar watch, was a walking, talking, flashing target.

After a long drive that felt less like a commute and more like a pilgrimage through the nine circles of traffic, I'd finally pulled into a spot outside "The Salty Siren," a bar that sounded like a pirate-themed restaurant for children but was, in fact, a haunt for locals with a penchant for mischief. I walked in, ordered a Scotch that probably cost more than the bartender's monthly rent, and tried my best to look inconspicuous. Which, for me, is about as easy as a flamingo trying to camouflage in a snowstorm.

My drink was a fiery amber liquid that tasted suspiciously like gasoline and regret. I sipped it slowly, trying to unwind, but the feeling of being watched was as heavy as a lead blanket. Every laugh seemed a little too loud, every whisper a little too pointed. I finished my drink, a small victory, and headed for the door, eager to escape this den of passive-aggressive hostility.

But the universe, it seemed, had other plans.

I stepped outside, my hand already in my pocket, keys jingling, ready to unlock my beautiful, shiny, pristine sedan. But where my car should have been, there was only an empty space. A perfectly, painfully empty space.

My car was gone.

My beautiful, brand-new, leather-scented baby was gone.

A cold, steely rage, a kind of fury I usually reserved for quarterly earnings reports and faulty printers, began to simmer in my gut. I looked at the spot again, as if willing my car to reappear.

It didn't.

The only thing that came back was the sound of distant, snickering laughter from inside the bar.

With a deep breath that tasted of injustice and a hint of gasoline from my last drink, I pushed the door open and re-entered the lion's den.

The air was thick with smoke and a collective smirk.

All eyes were on me, waiting for the expected outburst of panicked phone calls and impotent rage. I was, after all, just another city slicker who'd been bested by the good old boys.

But I would not play that game.

I walked to the bar, placed my left hand flat on the lacquered surface, and with my other, I flipped a gun into the air.

It was a beautiful, elegant thing, a collector's item I'd bought on a whim.

The gun you see in movies, not the kind you expect a businessperson to own. I caught it above my head without even looking, a trick I'd perfected in my youth, and fired a shot into the ceiling.

Plaster dust rained down like an unholy blizzard.

The bar went silent.

The snickering stopped.

The only sound was the high-pitched ringing in my ears and the echoing boom of the gunshot.

"Which of you stole my car?!" I yelled.

The sound of my voice, usually reserved for boardrooms and conference calls, was surprisingly forceful, almost primal.

No one answered. Just a sea of wide, terrified eyes. I'd gone from being a joke to a potential threat, and the shift in atmosphere was palpable.

I leaned on the bar, my voice dropping to a low, menacing whisper. "Alright," I said, "I'm going to have another drink, and if my car isn't back outside by the time I finish, I'm going to do what I did in Sydney! And I don't like to do what I did in Sydney!"

A ripple of unease spread through the crowd.

Some locals shifted restlessly, their bravado evaporating faster than a puddle in the Sahara.

The bartender, a man whose face was a roadmap of poor decisions, quickly poured me another Scotch, his hand shaking so badly some of the amber liquid splashed onto the bar.

I sipped it slowly, making a show of it.

Each sip was a countdown.

Each swallow a threat.

I could feel the eyes on me, the nervous energy in the room.

They didn't know what had happened in Sydney, but their imaginations were running wild.

Was it a bloodbath?

A rampage?

Had I burned a city to the ground?

The suspense was delicious.

Finally, I finished my drink.

I stood up, walked to the bar's door, opened it slightly, and peered outside.

And there it was.

My beautiful, shiny, pristine sedan returned to its original parking spot.

A small smile played on my lips. I turned back and nodded to the bartender and was about to leave when the bartender, his face a mask of morbid curiosity, wandered out from behind the bar.

"Say, Mister," he stammered, "before you go, what happened in Sydney?"

I paused, looked at him, and then at the bewildered faces of the other locals.

A grand story, a tale of heroic vengeance, was expected.

But I was a businessperson, not a storyteller.

"I had to walk home," I said, a faint smile on my lips.

And with that, I left them to their confusion and their stolen lessons, lighter in the wallet, but a lot richer in a story.

THE AGONY OF THE VERBOSE

I swear, sometimes I think my job title should be "Linguistic Decipherer and Sales Optimist," especially when I'm dealing with Dr. Phileas Foggins.

Now don't get me wrong, Phileas is a lovely woman, brilliant even.

She holds three doctorates, can quote obscure philosophical texts in their original Aramaic, and bakes a truly transcendent sourdough.

But when it comes to her prose?

Oh, sweet heavens, the vocabulary.

Her latest manuscript, The Ephemeral Gossamer of Sentient Quiescence, landed on my desk with a thud that echoed the collective sigh of our marketing department.

Phileas is a sesquipedalian, a lover of long words, to a degree that makes lexicographers weep tears of joy and normal readers weep tears of confusion.

Our sales figures for her previous works?

Let's just say they hovered somewhere between "negligible" and "statistically insignificant."

My boss, a man whose patience is as thin as an unstamped envelope, had given me an ultimatum: "Make it comprehensible, Finch, or we're commissioning a cat memoir."

I opened the document, braced for impact.

The first sentence alone was an intellectual marathon: "The crepuscular incandescence, a liminal effulgence of the nascent dawn, permeated the circumambient miasma, presaging the diurnal apotheosis with an ineffable chromatic spectrum."

My eye twitched.

I reread it, then again.

What in hell did that even mean?

"The sunrise was pretty?"

"Phileas," I'd said over our weekly video call, trying to sound as un-sarcastic as possible, "your descriptions are remarkably evocative. However, for the average reader, they might prove a tad complex."

She beamed, mistaking my thinly veiled criticism for praise.

"Ah, yes, Finch! One must eschew the commonplace, the pedestrian vernacular, for a lexical tapestry woven with the most exquisite, erudite threads! To condescend to brevity is to truncate the very soul of intellectual discourse!"

I chewed on my pen.

"Right. But we need more sales, Phileas. People are struggling with the lexical tapestry."

"Listen, we got a review that said, and I quote, *I think this book is about a lady who likes flowers, but honestly, I spent more time Googling words than reading.*"

Another simply read, 'My dictionary got a workout.'

Phileas merely sniffed.

"Philistines! They simply lack the perspicacity to appreciate the nuanced semantic dexterity of my authorial voice!"

My job, then, was to gently, painstakingly, almost imperceptibly, chisel away at her verbal Mount Everest.

My suggested edits often looked like this:

Phileas: "The protagonist's existential angst manifested as an anomie so profound it bordered on the cataleptic, an ontological void that prevented any semblance of quotidian felicity."

My suggestion: "The protagonist was very sad."

She'd invariably reject it with a note: "Finch, this distillation sacrifices the very essence of the intended emotional gravitas! It is an intellectual lobotomy!"

One particularly egregious paragraph described a character walking into a room. It was 150 words long and contained terms like "ambulatory perambulation," "chthonic substrata," and "unctuous propinquity."

I just wanted to write, "He walked into the room."

The breakthrough, if you could call it that, came not from persuasion, but from a rather desperate marketing meeting.

My boss, having given up on the "cat memoir," suggested we market Phileas's books as "Advanced Vocabulary Builders for the Discerning Reader."

We started including a free compact dictionary with every purchase.

The sales didn't exactly skyrocket, but they existed.

People weren't buying them as novels, but as linguistic challenges, ironic gifts, or conversation starters for particularly pretentious dinner parties.

One review, which I framed, declared: "Finally, a novel that makes Ulysses feel like a picture book! My SAT scores are up two hundred points, and I can now confidently use 'defenestration' in casual conversation."

So, I still edit Phileas's books.

I still occasionally bang my head on my desk when confronted with an adverbial phrase that sounds like a legal decree.

But now, when she sends me her new draft,

The Metaphysical Imbroglio of Convivial Contemplation, I just sigh, grab my red pen, and consider which dictionary to recommend to our increasingly niche, but undeniably dedicated, readership.

It's not the literary success story I envisioned, but at least Phileas is happy, and my dictionary skills are unparalleled.

DON'T YOU REMEMBER ME?

The sterile scent of disinfectant in the room differed from that of her perfume she used to wear around our home, but it did not distract me as I sat by her bed, the crisp white sheets a cruel canvas against her faded skin. Her eyes, once bright and dancing with mischief, now held a distant, unreadable gaze as they flickered over me.

"Hello, darling," I whispered, reaching for her hand.

It was frail, cool, and didn't respond with the familiar squeeze I'd known for fifty years. Her fingers lay limp in mine, eroded by time and illness.

She blinked.

"You're new, aren't you?" Her voice was a fragile thing, like a dry leaf skittering across pavement.

A sharp pain pierced my chest.

It was the same pain I felt every Tuesday and Thursday, the days I came to visit. Each time, I hoped, prayed, that this would be the day. The day her eyes would light up, the day she'd call me by name, the day she'd remember the spark that had ignited our entire world.

"No, my love. It's me, Robert. Your Robert. Your husband." I leaned closer, searching her eyes for any flicker of recognition.

She frowned.

Her gaze drifted around the small room, landing on the framed photograph on her bedside table—our wedding day, my arm around her waist, both of us beaming, utterly incandescent with joy.

"My husband?"

She looked from the photo to me, then back to the photo, as if trying to reconcile the two.

My heart ached.

This wasn't the first time.

It wouldn't be the last.

But each time, it felt like a fresh cut. I took a deep breath, forcing a gentle smile onto my face, the kind she always loved when I was trying to cheer her up.

I brought her hand to my lips, pressing a soft kiss to her knuckles.

"Yes," I said, my voice thick with emotion. "Don't you remember me?"

Her eyes searched mine again, a flicker—or was it just wishful thinking?—of something there, something almost familiar.

Then, her gaze softened, a faint, almost imperceptible smile touching her lips. "You have kind eyes," she said, her voice a little stronger. "I think I like you."

It wasn't the answer I craved.

But in that moment, it was enough.

More than enough.

Even if she didn't remember us, she still saw kindness.

And in her world, so fractured and uncertain, that was a connection I would cherish, a tiny spark of the love that still burned fiercely within me.

I squeezed her hand gently.

It was my silent promise I would never stop reminding her she is the love of my life.

ALONE IN THE KITCHEN

I've always considered myself a solivagant soul, a lone wolf in a world of packs, a single sock in a drawer full of pairs. This isn't because I dislike people, mind you, but more because, well, people complicate things.

Especially when those things involve my culinary experiments.

Take last Tuesday, for instance. I decided it was time to conquer the legendary Cheese Soufflé.

Now, a soufflé, as anyone who's ever glanced at a cooking show knows, is a delicate beast.

It requires precision, timing, and, apparently, a level of emotional support usually reserved for competitive gymnasts. But I scoffed at such notions. I, a seasoned veteran of solo instant ramen nights and the occasional microwave popcorn, was ready. My kitchen, usually a pristine testament to my aversion to cooking, became my arena.

The recipe, cheerfully titled "Effortless Elegance," seemed to mock me from the page.

It started innocently enough: "Melt butter, whisk in flour."

Easy peasy.

Then came the eggs.

"Separate six eggs, ensuring no yolk contaminates the whites."

This, I discovered, is a job for someone with surgeon-like steadiness, not a man whose hands occasionally vibrate when he's had too much coffee.

Three yolks perished in the valiant effort, turning otherwise innocent whites into yellow-tinged, unusable sludge.

"No matter," I muttered, retrieving more eggs. "A true solivagant makes do."

The "folding" process was next.

The instructions stated, "Gently fold the egg whites into the cheese mixture, as if caressing a cloud."

My technique, however, was less caress, more vigorous interrogation. The mixture deflated faster than a politician's promise.

I stirred, and I cursed, I even whispered sweet nothings to it, but the airy lightness had vanished, replaced by a dense, cheesy paste.

Still, optimism (or perhaps stubborn pride) prevailed.

I poured the stubbornly heavy mixture into the ramekin, ignoring the little voice in my head that sounded suspiciously like Gordon Ramsay screaming, "IT'S RAW, YOU DONKEY!"

Into the oven it went, a monument to my solo culinary ambition.

I watched through the oven door, a silent vigil.

For a glorious five minutes, nothing happened.

Then, a slow, hesitant rise.

"Aha! Effortless elegance, indeed!" I exclaimed, doing a little victory shimmy.

And then it happened.

Not a gentle puff, but a sudden, violent eruption.

The soufflé didn't rise; it launched. Cheese and eggy shrapnel splattered against the inside of the oven door, hissed off the heating elements, and even escaped through the vent, leaving a cheesy smear on the wall.

The gentle pop turned into a muffled THWUMP!

I stood there, covered in what looked suspiciously like a cheesy snowstorm, a single, deflated ramekin staring back at me from the oven's smoky interior.

My solivagant culinary journey had ended not with effortless elegance, but with a cleanup operation that required industrial-grade degreaser and a deep sense of shame. I guess some things are better shared, even if it's just the blame.

LEAVES, BRANCHES AND ROOTS

The scent of roasted coffee beans and warm croissants hung heavy in the air of "The Daily Grind," a cozy little cafe nestled on a bustling corner of Northport, New South Wales. Sunlight, filtered through the delicate lace curtains, painted shifting patterns on the checkered floor as Chloe stirred her latte, a faint sigh escaping her lips. Across from her, Maya, ever pragmatic, raised an eyebrow, her gaze sharp over the rim of her oversized ceramic mug.

"Another one, Chloe? I thought after Ben, you were taking a sabbatical from the male species." Maya asked with a hint of amusement in her voice.

"I was. I really, truly was. But then Mark happened. And he was different. He said all the right things, Maya. He actually listened. We had genuine conversations, not just about what we were watching on Netflix."

"And 'Mark happened' to last precisely three weeks before he decided he wasn't 'ready for anything serious'?" Maya finished without malice, simply stating a well-worn pattern.

"Honestly, Chloe, it's like you're collecting these fleeting encounters. Do you even want something serious? Or are you just hoping one of them will magically transform into Mr. Right?"

Chloe bristled slightly. "Of course I want something serious! I want stability. Partnership. Someone to share my life with. Isn't that what everyone wants?"

Chloe's voice dropped and continued: "But it just never lasts. It's always 'not the right time,' or 'I'm too busy with work,' or the classic 'you're amazing, but I'm exhausted, Maya. Are all men just temporary?"

Maya stirred her coffee thoughtfully.

"Not all men, no. But maybe the ones you're picking are. Or maybe you're not clear enough about what you're looking for from the start. We keep dating these guys who are perfectly fine for a few laughs, a few dinners, but then they evaporate the moment you hint at anything deeper. It's like we're always dealing with the ornamental foliage of a relationship, never getting to the sturdy trunk."

"Ornamental foliage," Chloe repeated, with a small, sad smile playing on her lips. "That's a clever way to put it. Beautiful for a season, then they just drop off."

Their conversation, though private in sentiment, had been carried in voices just loud enough to drift to the next table.

An elderly man with a gentle face framed by a halo of salt and pepper hair and kind eyes had been quietly sipping his coffee, ostensibly engrossed in his laptop. He cleared his throat softly, closed the laptop, and turned to them.

"Excuse me, young ladies. Please forgive an old man for eavesdropping. It was entirely unintentional, I assure you, but your conversation resonated with me."

He offered a small, apologetic smile. "I've lived a long time, and I've seen many things, especially with relationships."

Chloe and Maya exchanged a surprised glance, a little embarrassed but also intrigued. There was an earnestness in his gaze that disarmed them.

"You're both searching for something, and you're right; there are many types of, well, 'foliage,' as you put it. But perhaps the issue isn't the foliage itself but understanding what kind of tree you genuinely want to grow. You should focus on the type of relationship you want, not just the men who cross your path."

He leaned closer and his gaze shifting between them. "Relationships may come in three types, much like a tree."

Chloe and Maya leaned in, forgetting their initial awkwardness.

"First, there are the leaves. These relationships are around for a season. They are often beautiful, vibrant, full of life and colour, but they are inherently temporary. They come when the conditions are right, a shared interest, a moment of loneliness, a burst of passion, and then, when the season changes, they fall away. They enrich the tree for a time, provide shade, but they don't bear the weight of the years. You enjoy them while they are there, you learn from their brief presence, but you mustn't expect them to last."

Chloe nodded slowly, a flicker of recognition in her eyes. Mark, Ben, the others. They were all leaves.

"Then," the old man continued, holding up a second finger, "there are the branches. These are stronger than the leaves, certainly. They stay longer, grow thicker, and can even bear fruit. These are the relationships that feel more substantial, that weather a few storms, that you invest in, believing they might be the ones to deeply hold. You build a life around them; you share dreams; you lean on them. But even branches, for all their strength and longevity, can eventually break. Something will cause them to snap, and when they do, it's painful. It reshapes the tree, leaving a void that takes time to heal. You might have several branches throughout your life, and each teaches you something profound, even in its breaking."

Maya thoughtfully tapped her mug.

She had a few significant relationships that fit that description, long-term partners who had been integral to her life for years, only for them to eventually diverge or fracture under pressure. The pain of those breaks was still a dull ache.

"And finally," the man said, a warm, expansive smile returning to his face, "there are the root relationships."

His eyes softened, distant, as if gazing at a cherished memory.

"These are the ones that take hold forever. You must trust me when I say these are not flashy or even immediately apparent. These roots buried deep, providing unseen nourishment and unwavering support. Without you sensing it, they will become your foundation, the lifeblood of the relationship. These relationships are the ones that will anchor you. They will help you find your strength from the deepest parts of your entire being. They can, will, withstand the most intense moments, the fiercest storms, and the longest droughts. These roots, they grow with you, connect with you, and become an inseparable part of who you are. These roots are uncommon, precious, and often incredibly quiet in their power. They offer you three wonderful things: patience, nurturing, and an unshakeable commitment."

"My wife," he said, his voice barely a whisper, "she was my roots. For twenty-eight years I knew her before she passed away on June 10, 2025. She anchored me. So, ask yourselves, what kind of relationship are you truly seeking? Are you happy collecting beautiful leaves, seeking sturdy branches, or are you ready to cultivate the roots?"

He pushed himself slowly up from his chair.

"Thank you for letting an old man ramble."

As he gathered his laptop and with one last, kind glance, walked out of "The Daily Grind," leaving the soft chime of the bell in his wake.

Chloe and Maya sat in silence, the lingering scent of coffee and the faint echo of the bell filling the void left by the old man's departure.

The clatter of cups, the murmur of other conversations, all seemed to restart after he left.

Chloe was the first to speak, her voice hushed.

"Dammit Maya. It is all in front of us. Leaves... branches... roots..."

She looked at Maya, her eyes wide with a new clarity. "I think I've been so focused on avoiding the next leaf falling, I haven't even considered what kind of tree I'm trying to grow."

Maya nodded slowly, a thoughtful frown creasing her brow. "And I've been so afraid of another branch breaking, I might have stopped looking for the roots altogether."

She picked up her spoon and began stirring her now-cool coffee, not out of habit, but as if turning over new thoughts.

"He's right, isn't he? It's not just about who joins us, but what we're willing to create together."

The old widower's conversation had evoked something in their minds. Chloe and Maya now felt that the meaningful distinction between something temporary, like a leaf, something reliable like a branch, and something permanent like a root.

As they as quietly and continued sipping their coffee, they smiled and looked at each other, knowing the words of a kind man had opened their hearts on how to look for new relationships in the future.

ESCAPE REDUX*

Barry Saunders was tired of his lady, bless her heart. They'd been together so long they were less like a couple and more like two worn-out bookends holding up a single, very boring encyclopedia.

As she snored, a sound he'd long since integrated into his white noise machine, he read the online Sydney Morning Herald. A small, unassuming ad in the personal/classified columns caught his eye.

A woman was looking for a man who liked mojitos, who enjoyed getting caught in the rain, wasn't into yoga, and had half a brain. She wanted a lover to meet her in the dunes on the cape for a midnight rendezvous. Barry didn't think about his lady.

He knew it was mean, but he had an idea. He'd spice things up. He'd place an ad of his own.

His response — a clumsy verse he was convinced was sheer poetry — read:

I like mojitos and getting caught in the rain.
I'm not into health food; I'm into champagne.
I've got to meet you by tomorrow noon and cut through all this red tape.
At a bar called The Thirsty Troll, where we'll plan our escape.

And I'll be wearing a yellow bow tie and a red rose on my lapel.

He imagined a line of women, a whole conga line of them, trying to catch his eye, each one a different and exciting adventure.

He fell asleep with a devious grin on his face.

The next day, Barry, sporting a bow tie the colour of a school bus and a rose so red it looked like it was bleeding, confidently walked into The Thirsty Troll.

The bar was packed.

He scanned the room, looking for a glimpse of a hopeful woman, but all he saw were men.

Men of all shapes and sizes.

Some were bald, some were bearded, and one looked suspiciously like the Northport's mayor.

All of them were wearing bright yellow bow ties.

All of them had a single red rose pinned to their lapels.

A husky guy with a beard so thick it looked like it could hold a schooner of beer walked up to Barry.

"You're the one who likes mojitos?" he said, a hopeful glint in his eye. "I've got a complete garden of roses on my back patio."

Barry's jaw went slack.

Another man, this one in a business suit, stepped forward. "I'm not much into health food either," he said with a wink. "Champagne's more my style. Let's talk about our escape plan."

Barry looked around again.

The entire bar was a sea of yellow and red, a bizarre garden of hopeful men all looking for an escape with a mojito-loving stranger.

Barry mumbled something about needing to use the toilet and then bolted for the exit, leaving his bow tie and rose on the bar as a sacrifice to the bizarre turn of events.

He returned home to his worn-out lady, a woman he suddenly appreciated more than ever.

She was snoring, but now it sounded less like a white noise machine and more like a symphony.

And as he snuck back into bed, a quiet thought formed in his mind: perhaps their worn-out routine wasn't so bad after all.

*Apologies to Rupert Holmes

BUY THREE AND GET THE FOURTH FREE

You'd think buying tyres would be a straightforward affair. You know—walk in, pick the black round things that stop your car from kissing the asphalt too intimately, and leave. But no. Not with me. I have a magical ability to turn the simplest errand into a monumental exercise with a laugh track.

My Holden Trax had been squeaking, wobbling, and threatening to launch me into roadside shrubbery, so I bit the bullet and decided it was time for tyres. Three of them. The fourth was perfectly fine, practically glowing with smug health.

I roll into "Tread Masters Tyre Emporium" and I am greeted by the service manager. He's the bloke who wears a polo shirt with his name, Gary, stitched on it and a smile that could sell snow to penguins.

"G'day, mate! Looking for tyres?"

"No, Gary, I came here to buy a mattress," I replied.

I thought it was funny.

Gary didn't.

"Yes," I sighed, "three tyres."

He blinks at me like I'd just asked for a single shoelace. "Three?"

"Yes, one-two-three." I held up my fingers as if I were teaching kindergarten.

Gary's grin returns, shark-like.

"Perfect timing, mate! We've got a deal right now: buy three tyres and get the fourth one free!"

I swear, somewhere in the back of the store, a cash register rang in triumph.

"Ah," I said, "but you see, Gary, I only need three."

"Right," he says, clapping his hands. "You'll get four then. Brilliant deal!"

"Hold on," I replied. "What happens to the fourth?"

"You get it for free."

"Yes, but I don't need it. My fourth tyre is in excellent condition. It does yoga. Drinks mango smoothies. Meditates. I don't want to replace it."

Gary shrugs. "Well then, you'll have a spare."

I looked him dead in the eye.

"I've got a spare in the boot, Gary, so just give me three tyres and hand me the $300 for the fourth in cash. Everybody wins."

You'd think I'd suggested a blood sacrifice from the way he recoiled.

"We can't do that, mate."

"Why not? You were going to give me a tyre worth $300. I'm politely requesting the monetary equivalent. No one loses here, Gary."

He adjusts his glasses.

"Sir, that's not how promotions work."

"Look," I lean in, conspiratorial, "between you and me, a tyre is only useful if it's on a car. Otherwise, it's just a black rubber coffee table."

Gary crosses his arms. "Rules are rules."

That's when the negotiations began.

"Gary," I start, "think of it like this: you've budgeted for me to walk away with four tyres, correct?"

"Yes."

"But I don't want four. If I take three and cash, you've still spent the same amount but made me happier. Happy customers return. That's how you build loyalty. Word-of-mouth. Future sales. A legacy, Gary."

He blinks. "We don't do legacies. We sell tyres."

"Gary," I whisper, gripping the counter like I'm confessing to a crime, "I'm a man of limited means. I am a retiree. My tyres are almost bald. My wife just passed away, but she had a look at them before going up to the great raceway in the sky and she said they look like vinyl records. Do you know what it's like to hydroplane on the M5 while a semi-trailer breathes down your neck?"

His lip twitches.

Sympathy?

A laugh?

Hard to tell.

"Still can't give you cash."

"Fine," I say, slapping my card on the counter. "Charge me for three, and instead of the fourth tyre, give me $300 worth of meat trays from the Meat Man across the street."

"Sir, we don't do butcher cross-promotions."

"Then a voucher? A fuel card? Three hundred dollars' worth of Lotto tickets?"

Gary shakes his head like a man who's seen too much.

A woman behind me, clearly entertained, leans in.

"Mate, take the fourth tyre. Stick it in the backyard. Grow potatoes in it."

"Not helping, stranger," I think to myself.

"Listen," I say, "you give me three tyres, and I'll write a glowing online review. I'll mention your smile, your customer service, your ability to resist nonsense. People will flock here."

Gary smirks.

"Or I can sell you four tyres, and you can keep your review."

Touché.

By now, a small audience has gathered.

An even older man than I am now sneaks up behind me and is openly eating popcorn he clearly didn't buy there. Two apprentices have stopped pretending to shuffle tyres around and are just watching us like it's the heavyweight title fight.

I double down.

"Gary, it's the principle. Why give me something I don't need when you could give me something I do? It's efficiency! It's justice! It's..."

"It's not happening."

That's when inspiration struck.

"Fine," I say. "Give me three tyres and one wheelbarrow tyre. You know, for the garden."

Gary blinks again.

I think I broke him.

"We don't stock wheelbarrow tyres."

"Then give me three tyres and a beanbag. Or three tyres and a steering wheel cover. Something of equal value!"

He sighs, pinching the bridge of his nose.

"Sir, do you want the deal or not?"

I puff out my chest. "I want justice, Gary."

In the end, of course, I lost.

I walked out with four tyres.

My Trax looked like it was wearing four brand-new pairs of sneakers, and my wallet was $900 lighter.

But I had the last laugh.

Two weeks later, I put the fourth tyre on Facebook Marketplace: "Brand New Tyre, Never Used. $250 OBO."

Did I make my $300 back?

No.

Did I spend every pickup inquiry explaining why I was only selling one tyre? Yes.

"Why only one?" people asked.

"Because I argued with a man named Gary and lost." I'd reply.

And that, dear reader, is how a simple trip to buy three tyres became my proudest failure.

Somewhere, Gary is still telling the story of the lunatic who tried to cash out a free tyre like it was a poker chip.

And me?

Every time I see that perfectly fine tyre still sitting in my garage, glaring at me like an abandoned puppy, I whisper, "We could have been $300 richer."

THE MICROWAVE AT NASA

My sister, Clara, believes she's a genius. Not in the "got a PhD" way, but in the "I once fixed the toaster by hitting it with a spoon; therefore, I could probably run NASA."

The problem is, I don't think Clara actually understands the concept of genius, or spoons, or toasters for that matter.

One Saturday morning, she came into the kitchen holding her phone and wearing that smirk that always signals disaster.

"I just read about something called the Dunning-Kruger effect," she announced, plopping down at the table. "Apparently, people who know the least think they know the most. Good news: I'm immune."

I almost choked on my cereal.

"That is literally the opposite of what the effect means." She waved me off.

"No, no, I get it. People think they're smart, but really, they're not. But I am smart, so I can't possibly have it. That's how you know I don't."

This was like hearing someone say, "I'm not arrogant because I'm perfect."

To prove her brilliance, Clara decided to "fix" the microwave, which, by the way, was not broken.

She dragged a screwdriver out of the drawer, opened the microwave door, and announced: "This is basically just a small oven that's confused about its identity. If I recalibrate the frequency modulators..."

"There are no modulators," I said.

"Clara, you don't even know what that word means."

"Of course I do," she shot back. "It means the thing that modulates. Duh."

That's when she actually unscrewed the handle. The entire handle came off in her hand.

"See?" she said, beaming. "Now the airflow is optimised."

"Clara. You broke the only part that lets us open it." I said, pinching the bridge of my nose.

She stared at the handle, then at the microwave, then at me.

"Well, maybe they designed it wrong in the first place."

That's the thing about the Dunning-Kruger effect. You can't argue someone out of it. The less they know, the more confident they are.

So now when I want to use the microwave, I need pliers. Clara, however, has been telling everyone she "streamlined" the kitchen appliances.

Last night she looked at me proudly and said, "You know, if NASA ever called me, I'd probably help them save a billion dollars."

And I said, "Yeah, Clara. Just make sure they don't let you near the microwave in Mission Control."

GARY

My name is Glormag, a name that, I must admit, is rather misleading. It conjures images of fire-breathing, village-plundering, and the general smiting of all that is good and green.

I suppose I can't blame the village folk for their vivid imaginations. I have horns that could double as coat racks, scales the colour of a stormy sea, and a set of fangs that, while excellent for tearing into a roasted leg of lamb, make people scream and faint.

But the truth, the boring truth, is that I am a connoisseur of fine pastries and a dabbler in the delicate art of soufflé-making.

My lair is on the side of Mount Crag, is not filled with piles of plundered gold or the bones of fallen heroes. It's filled with monstrously large cookbooks, a vast collection of decorative spools of yarn (I'm quite a knitter), and a colossal, custom-built kitchen mixer that sounds like a collapsing mountain range when in use. Which is a major source of misunderstanding.

The other day, I was attempting a recipe for an Elderberry and Roasted Almond Soufflé.

It's a notoriously difficult dish, requiring the perfect balance of egg whites and delicate folding. I had just reached the crucial folding stage, a dance of precision and brute force. My mixer whirred to life, its churning blades creating a deep, resonant hum that vibrated the very stones of the mountain.

From my perspective, it was the sweet music of culinary creation.

From the valley below, it was apparently a harbinger of the end times.

The first rumblings began, and I could hear the panicked shouts from the village of Oak Haven.

"The Earth Trembles! Glormag has awakened!" they cried.

I sighed, sloshing a bit of batter onto my snout.

No, friends. Glormag is attempting to master the art of leavening.

A subtle but important distinction.

I was so focused on my batter that I didn't notice the approach of the "heroes" until they were practically at my front door.

The first to burst into my kitchen was Sir Reginald the Resplendent, a knight so shiny he could blind you with a well-timed head turn. He held a sword aloft, its tip trembling.

Behind him were Bartholomew the Brash, a wizard whose magical robes were at least two sizes too large, and a young archer with a serious-looking bow and a very serious-looking expression, Elara.

They took one look at me—my scales slick with goo, my fangs bared in concentration—and the scene before them.

The cavern floor was a disaster of flour dust and spilled sugar.

My massive mixer was churning away.

The soufflé batter was bubbling ominously, and a large blob had oozed over the side of the bowl, dripping onto the floor with a rhythmic plop.

"Behold the creature of prophecy! The Elderberry Demon, spewing forth its vile, world-ending sludge!" Sir Reginald bellowed, his voice cracking with fear.

I blinked, confused.

World-ending sludge?

It was just batter.

Delicious elderberry-scented batter.

I tried to speak, but my tongue was too thick with a chewy elderberry.

"G-ggl... glorp?" I managed, which to them probably sounded like a guttural threat.

Bartholomew, the wizard, shrieked and began fumbling with a small, glowing orb.

"I shall conjure a fireball!" he declared, his voice a high-pitched squeak. He tossed the orb, which hit the wall and fizzled out with a pathetic little puff of steam, leaving a wet patch on the stone.

He sighed with relief. "Well, at least it wasn't a lightning bolt this time."

Elara, the archer, took out an arrow, her serious expression even more serious now.

"I'm not afraid of you, beast! Your reign of terror ends now!" she said, her voice shaking just a little.

My heart sank.

This was a classic misunderstanding.

They saw the mess and assumed the worst.

I held up my giant, clawed hands in a gesture of peace. "Wait! It's just a soufflé!" I tried to explain, but my voice, a low rumble even when I'm excited, just made them flinch.

Sir Reginald charged, and he swung his sword, aiming for the mixer. "I shall destroy the source of your evil!" he shouted.

This was a culinary crisis!

That mixer was a one-of-a-kind model, forged by a grumpy gnome I knew.

I had to stop him.

I lunged forward, not to attack, but to intercept his swing.

My massive, clumsy hand knocked the sword aside; my elbow slammed into the side of the mixer bowl.

A geyser of purple batter erupted, soaring into the air like a volcanic plume.

It descended upon the three heroes in a gooey shower.

Bartholomew shrieked as a glob of batter landed on his face, momentarily blinding him. Elara let out a surprised gasp as her serious bow was coated in the sticky, sweet mixture. And Sir Reginald took the full brunt of it.

He stood frozen, a statue of terror, as the purple soufflé batter completely encased his shiny helmet.

He wobbled for a moment, then toppled over with a metallic clang, his armour now a hilarious shade of lavender.

I stood there, covered in my mess, feeling a mix of dread and embarrassment.

The jig was up, as the saying goes.

They would surely see me as the Soufflé-Smiting Monster now.

But then, a small, muffled sound came from inside Sir Reginald's helmet.

"Is that elderberry?" came the faint, bewildered voice. He peeled a piece of the batter off his helmet's visor. "And roasted almonds?"

Bartholomew, who had wiped his face clean, sniffed the air. "It smells delicious!" he said, his terror replaced by a look of sheer confusion.

Elara, the archer, lowered her bow. She looked from me, the giant, supposedly evil monster, to the giant, obviously kitchen mixer, and then back to the oozing trail of batter. She let out a snort, then a giggle, then full-blown laughter.

"You weren't trying to destroy the world. You were just trying to bake a cake!" she said, wiping a tear from her eye.

I nodded, feeling a flush of pride. "A soufflé, actually. It's a unique process."

Sir Reginald, having finally pried his helmet off, stood up, his face a mix of purple goo and deep embarrassment.

"I see," he said, looking at the industrial-strength mixer with new respect. "My apologies, Glormag. We assumed the worst."

I waved a hand dismissively. "Happens all the time. My name doesn't help. It's a curse, really. I prefer Gary."

The three of them exchanged glances.

They were no longer heroes facing a legendary monster.

They were just three people who had just been splattered with a monster's baking project.

I gestured toward the inside of my lair.

"Well, the soufflé is ruined, of course. Too much agitation. But I have some fresh ginger biscuits and a kettle of chamomile tea. Would you care to rest a bit?"

They hesitated, then nodded.

We sat around my massive stone table, sipping tea from mugs that were the size of their heads, and they listened, enthralled, as I explained the nuances of gluten-free flour and the delicate art of separating egg whites without tearing a yolk.

Sir Reginald, a man who had faced dragons and griffins without a flinch, confessed that his greatest baking triumph was a perfectly toasted slice of bread. Bartholomew the wizard admitted his genuine passion was for conjuring little birds out of thin air. And Elara, the serious archer, turned out to be an excellent conversationalist.

In the end, we parted as friends.

They promised to spread the word that Glormag the Grotesque was no longer a monster, but a misunderstood pastry chef.

I knew it would be a hard sell.

Old habits die hard, especially when your village is built on tales of monsters and mayhem.

But as I went back to my kitchen, now with a new recipe for gingerbread cookies, I felt a little lighter.

It's a tough world for a monster who just wants to bake in peace. But every once in a while, you find a few humans who will give peace a chance.

And maybe try a bite of your delicious soufflé and become your friend.

AGAIN

My name is Barry, and I am a rock. I'm a good, solid rock, about the size of a grumpy wombat, and I've been sitting here on the edge of this bush track for, well, for a very long time.

I don't count the days.

It's a human thing, that.

From my vantage point, time is measured in the searing heat of the sun, the gentle sweep of the afternoon breeze, and the slow, slow crawl of lichens across my ancient surface.

I've seen many creatures navigate this trail.

The wallabies, for instance, are marvels of bouncing grace.

They spot me from a long way off, and in one fluid hop of a flicky tail and a nimble jump, they're over me and gone, barely making a sound.

The emus, with their long, gangly legs, seem to know my every contour. They simply step around me, their gaze serene. And the wombats — ah, the wombats — they approach with a purposeful waddle, nudge me with a sniff of profound analysis, and then, if the mood strikes them, they might try to burrow under me before shuffling off.

They never, not once, stumble.

And then there are the humans.

My first encounter with a human was a truly bewildering affair.

A young bloke came shuffling down the path, his face buried in a small, glowing rectangle he held in his hands. He was making a series of dings and whistles, and his attention was clearly elsewhere.

As he approached me, I braced myself for the elegant detour that every other creature seemed to manage.

He didn't detour.

He hit me fair and square with his left foot.

A sudden, high-pitched "G'DAY!" split the quiet air.

He performed what I can only describe as a clumsy, arm-waving ballet, his glowing rectangle flying from his hand and clattering onto the dry dirt.

He landed in a heap, his knees scraping the ground, and for a moment, he just lay there, a tangle of limbs and bruised pride.

He then slowly rose, dusted himself off, and shot a glare at me as if I had leapt out and tripped him.

I am a rock.

I don't leap.

I am not the problem.

He picked up his device, grumbled something about "bloody rocks," and continued on his way, limping slightly.

I thought, "Well, that was odd, but at least he's learned his lesson."

That's the part that I simply cannot understand.

The part that separates humanity from every other creature I have ever had the pleasure of being a rock next to.

A few hours later, the same human came back down the trail.

My stony heart beat with a sort of morbid anticipation.

I had a feeling.

He was still looking at his glowing rectangle.

He was still making chirping noises.

It was like he had a memory that lasted all of three feet and two hours. I tried to mentally project a warning: "Look up, mate! I'm still here! I'm a rock! Don't do it again!"

But alas, I am a rock, and my powers of mental projection are limited.

He hit me with the same foot.

The "AUGH!" was more of a weary groan this time, a sound of profound exasperation.

He flailed with a tired familiarity, his arms already a blur of desperation before he even hit the ground.

He fell into the same patch of dust he had landed in before. He lay there for a long moment, this time just shaking his head.

He looked at me, a flicker of something new in his eyes—not just anger, but a kind of resigned bewilderment, as if to say, "Why me? Why you?"

I wanted to say, "Why? Because you are the only animal on this continent that can trip over the same rock twice."

The wallabies remember me.

The emus remember me.

The wombats remember me (or at least my stubbornness).

But humans?

They seem to exist in a perpetual state of amnesia when it comes to the humble, unmoving obstacles of the world.

They will complain about life's insignificant problems, but they are the only ones who seem to keep walking straight into them.

It's a baffling, humbling thing to witness from my solid, unmoving existence. And now, as a new human with a similar glowing rectangle approaches, I feel a weary sense of déjà vu.

I have a feeling I'm about to witness a human doing something only humans can do.

Again.

WINNING

My name is Miranda, and even when I was a child, I've had a second voice in my head. Mind you, it was a whisper or a fleeting thought, but a presence.

A deep, resonant hum just behind my eyes.

I call it the Shadow.

It's not the voice of madness, not in the screaming, straitjacket kind of way.

It's the voice of my most brutal, honest, and frankly, selfish self.

It's the part of me that sees the easy, destructive path and finds it far more appealing than the long, virtuous one.

I am a botanist, and I spend my days charming life from seeds, meticulously charting the growth of fragile seedlings, and marvelling at the delicate unfurling of new leaves. My life is filled with meticulous order and careful cultivation; however, the Shadow wants to burn the garden down to see what grows in the ashes.

For years, I've kept it at bay, ignoring its barbed suggestions.

When a colleague would take credit for my research, the Shadow would whisper, "Spill coffee on their keyboard. Sabotage their presentation."

And I would instead bite my tongue and correct them politely in the next staff meeting.

When a friend would cancel plans on me for the third time, the Shadow would snarl, "Block their number. Tell everyone what a flake they are."

And I would instead send a simple, "Hope you're okay!"

It was an exhausting, unending war.

I felt like I was constantly wrestling with my own hands, my feet, my very own heart. But the greatest battle began with Julian.

Julian was more than a colleague; he was my partner in the field.

We had spent two years on a project to develop a drought-resistant strain of wildflowers, a painstaking process of cross-pollination and genetic modification.

The project was the culmination of my life's work, a green dream I had been chasing since I was a child. Julian, with his simple charm and brilliant mind, had been a perfect collaborator.

Or so I thought.

The day our final paper was accepted for the most prestigious journal in our field, he called me, his voice a giddy mess of excitement. "It's published, Miranda! We did it!"

"We did it!" I echoed, my heart soaring.

But then came the email.

The one with a link to the article. I clicked it, my hands trembling with anticipation, and there, at the top, was the author's list: "Julian Vance." And underneath, in small, almost invisible font, "with research help from Miranda Reed."

The world went silent.

The air in my office grew heavy and thick, and a chilling cold spread through my veins.

And then, the Shadow, usually a low hum, roared to life.

"See?" it hissed, its voice a sharp-edged thing made of broken glass. "I told you. They're all the same. They'll take everything and leave you with nothing. Now you see the truth."

I slumped into my chair, staring at the screen.

The polite, measured words of my professional life were gone, replaced by a storm of rage.

The Shadow was right.

All those times I had let things go, had taken the high road, had been a fool. Julian had played me.

He had used me.

"Do it," the Shadow urged, its voice like a warm, seductive poison.

"You know his new research. You know his weak points. One anonymous email to the department head. One perfectly placed comment on a public forum. You could ruin him. You could show them what a mistake they made. You could take back what's yours."

The suggestions were so clear, so simple.

Vindictive satisfaction paved my path before me.

I could picture Julian's face as he read the accusations.

I could imagine the quiet whispers in the hallways.

I felt the heat of fury building in my chest, a fire that promised to burn away the pain and humiliation.

For the first time, I wanted to listen to the Shadow. I wanted to let it out, to let it run free.

I stood up, my fists clenched and walked to my laptop.

My fingers hovered over the keyboard. Julian's email address.

The subject line: "Regarding Julian Vance's unethical practices."

The words were already forming in my mind.

My office overlooks the campus greenhouse, and looking through the glass, I could see the wildflower seedlings.

Tiny, vulnerable things, just beginning to sprout.

They were my work.

My legacy.

I had nurtured something with painstaking effort, not with anger or spite.

The Shadow saw my hesitation, and its voice grew louder, more frantic. "Don't be weak! This is your chance! He deserves it!"

"Yes," I whispered to myself, "he deserves it."

And that was the moment everything changed.

I saw the truth not through the Shadow's eyes, but through my own.

He deserved it. And I, Miranda Reed, deserved better.

I deserved a life where my triumphs were built on my merit, not on the destruction of others.

I deserved to be proud of my work, and this path would make me nothing but bitter.

The Shadow's voice wavered.

It wasn't a roar anymore, but a petulant whine. "You're just going to let him win?"

I took my hands off the keyboard.

"No," I said, my voice steady, "I'm not fighting him. I'm fighting you."

The realisation settled over me, not as a thunderclap, but as a quiet, profound understanding.

The Shadow wasn't an external demon, but a part of me I had been trying to suppress, to starve out of existence.

But you can't kill a part of yourself. You can only learn to live with it.

I closed the laptop and walked to the greenhouse.

I felt the familiar hum of the Shadow, but this time, it was different.

It was still there, a low, grumbling presence, but I wasn't fighting it. I was acknowledging it.

"I see you," I thought. "I know you want to lash out. I know you're angry. And that's okay. But we will not do that."

I picked up a watering can and tended my seedlings.

My hands, which had been clenched with rage, were now gently nurturing the fragile shoots.

The act was a quiet promise to me.

I would not let anger be my harvest. I would not let bitterness be my final yield.

The following morning, I composed a letter to the journal's editorial board. In it, I presented the evidence methodically, allowing the facts to tell their own story. I had chosen the more difficult route, one that demanded patience and faith in an institution that had already let me down.

The Shadow grumbled, but it was a low, defeated sound.

I don't know what will happen.

Maybe nothing.

Maybe the journal will ignore my letter, and Julian will get away with it.

But I know this: I am not my rage. I am not my bitterness. I am a woman who cultivates life, who believes in fresh growth.

And that, I realised, was a choice I had to make every single day.

The battle was not with the world, but with me.

And for the first time, I felt like I was winning.

ABOUT THE AUTHOR

José F. Nodar is an Australian-Cuban author, reviewer, and literary entrepreneur based in Spring Farm, NSW. He is the founder of Quick Story Tales Online and World Book Reviews, initiatives supporting and promoting both emerging and established authors worldwide.

José's writing blends humour, sentiment, and quiet realism, often drawing from the landscapes and community spirit of regional New South Wales. His fiction, including Whispers from My Wife, The Northport Coffee Group, and Stories to Share with My Partner Collection, explores universal themes of love, loss, and rediscovery.

When not writing, José can be found reading at a local café, walking along Spring Farm's footpaths, or championing local authors and creative groups through interviews and newsletters.

Please visit https://worldbookreviews.com.au/ and let me know what you thought of this book of short stories and poetry.

Good, bad, or indifferent, I will always welcome your honest opinion.

Send me an email at info@jfnodar.com.au

Thank you for your purchase!

Other books by José F. Nodar:

Novels in English

The Danny Monk Trilogy

Books, Pens & Larceny
Mending Hearts at Crystal Cove
A Love Finally Spoken

The Mallard E. Benson Trilogy

The Girl Who Didn't Come Home
The Ones That Got Away
The Ghost We Owe

Mystery

The Ghost Detective's First Case
The Northport Coffee Group

Romance

The Teacher's Assistant
A Night of Love
Maybe This Is Everything
Love in Stereo
When Love Remembers

Science Fiction & Fantasy

The Compass Legacy
The Universe Between Us
The Time Bus
The Last Light of Aurethis

Children

The Hamster Who Whispered Back

Humour

SEX

Collections of Stories and Poetry

Stories to Share with My Partner Book 1
Stories to Share with My Partner Book 2
Stories to Share with My Partner Book 3
Stories to Share with My Partner Book 4
Stories to Share with My Partner Book 5
Stories to Share with My Partner Book 6
Stories to Share with My Partner Book 7
Stories to Share with My Partner Book 8
Stories to Share with My Partner Book 9
Stories to Share with My Partner Book 10
Stories to Share with My Partner Book 11
Stories to Share with My Partner Book 12

Anthologies of Stories and Poetry

Quick Stories & Poems Volume I
Quick Stories & Poems Volume 2
Quick Stories & Poems Volume 3

Libros en Español

La Trilogía de Danny Monk

Un Amor Expresado
Reparando Corazones en Crystal Cove
Un Amor Finalmente Declarado

Colecciones de Cuentos y Poemas

Cuentos Para Compartir con Mi Pareja Libro 1
Cuentos Para Compartir con Mi Pareja Libro 2
Cuentos Para Compartir con Mi Pareja Libro 3

Ciencia Ficción y Fantasía

El Autobús del Tiempo